Y0-BRR-238

At The Very Beginning

"You saw it too, didn't you? The man in the Saint Arbucks who collapsed all of a sudden?"

She gasped and almost dropped the note -- this note had obviously been left for her. Steadying herself on the locker door, she took another look at the note. It had been typed, which only added to its mystery. Whoever this was who sent the note didn't want to be revealed just yet.

"You don't know who I am yet. And that's okay. Because I don't know you yet either. All I know is that we both saw the same thing yesterday morning, and nobody else will back up our claim. If you're not scared, you can meet me on the roof after school. I'll be waiting there if you want to discuss this further. I don't have answers, but at least now you know you're not crazy." There was one final note at the bottom. *"Also, I know you saw what I saw because you announced it to your entire homeroom class, Word spreads fast."*

Emily Ann Imes

The Mystery of Taconum Carnival
Rhythm Buster 200X: Blue Impulse
Steel Angel
Almond Dust
Reclaim

The Dvorak Series
0: Dvorak Classic
1: The Dealey Five (serialization)
2: Begins Serialization December 2013

d-VOR-ak

The Dvorak Series Book 0

by Emily Ann Imes

*To Corey —
have fun in
Rochester!
Emily Ann Imes*

SOSI/Cap-Sid Broadcasters

New York, NY   Zanesville, OH

The interior and exterior of this book is © Emily Ann Imes 2013. All rights reserved. This book, or parts thereof, may not be reproduced in any way, shape, or form without specific written permission from the author/publisher. The scanning, uploading, and distribution of this book via the Internet or other means is prohibited, illegal, and punishable by law save for authorized electronic editions. Your support of the author's rights is appreciated.

For legal permission, please contact:

Emily Ann Imes

1850 Aspen Dr.

Zanesville, OH 43701

This book is printed on white paper, 5.5X8.5. The font is printed in Times New Roman. Dvorak's logo is in American Typewriter.

Cover photo by Milton "MyL10" Ian Piñeiro.

The "Saint Arbucks" name is used as a parody and no trademark infringement is intended. Any similarity to any actual coffeeshops is purely coincidental.

There's more to this world than meets the eye.

You've probably heard that said many times before, but it is true, reflected in our world, the media, and everywhere around us. Surprises behind every corner, expecting the unexpected...but what if even the most routine of days could not be taken for granted? The world we live in is prone to excitement and surprise and wonder and fear, but what does it really mean to feel those emotions? What is this world, life, reality?

The answer you will soon find out for yourself.

1

Saint Arbucks

So where was that blasted cup holder?

She pushed aside several old glasses, cups, plates, even digging around in the silverware for a few moments. She let out a sigh, coming up short. It had to be in here somewhere, as the dishes had just been done this past weekend. If this took much longer, she was going to miss her train.

Behind the dishwasher...up on top of the cereal boxes...past the cans of tuna...there! She grabbed the plastic red cup holder and stuffed it into her white duffel bag. With one more adjustment, she made sure her duffel was good to go and she was off, down four flights of stairs and out onto the cold morning on 181st Street.

It was a short subway ride downtown to her school, an academy on the Upper West Side that her parents paid extra for each month. Today was January 7th, the first day back to school after the winter holiday recess. She had left early enough to stop at Saint Arbucks Coffee and grab her favorite drink: a medium sized chai with an extra shot of espresso. There were times that she could meet her friends there, but today would be a solo trip. The cup holder search would have thrown her morning's routine off anyway, and her friends had already left her neighborhood by the time she got out her door.

She walked into the Saint Arbucks Coffeeshop on the

corner of 72nd and Broadway exactly at 7:16 in the morning, per her smartphone, which she was constantly glued to (even in class). The shop was unusually quiet for this time in the morning, and there weren't a lot of people sitting at the tables, though there was a nice long line (as usual).

After waiting in line for what seemed like hours (as it always did at that time in the morning), she got to the cash register and ordered her chai, then ducked into the bathroom while the chai was being made for a quick morning post subway makeup checkup. She brushed a few stray strands of dark brown hair out of her chocolate eyes, honing in on the mascara through the small mirror, harsh ceiling lights magnifying her every feature. Her short stature meant that she had to stand on her tiptoes to get it just right. She balanced herself with her left hand while applying with her right hand. Her duffel bag sat on the trash can, precariously perched much like its owner. With one last swipe, she fell back on her heels and straightened out her starched white uniform shirt, making sure it covered her all the way to her waist and the seams of her blue skirt. With a satisfied sigh, she smiled at herself in the mirror just as she heard her name called outside the bathroom by the barista.

She grabbed her red winter coat from the knob and ran outside the bathroom, going up to the counter. "That's me," she said as she reached back for her duffel to get her cup holder. But the duffel wasn't there – she had left it in the bathroom. Horrified, she looked behind her just as the bathroom door closed, somebody else occupying the room. Drat. How was she going to get her duffel back now?

"Excuse me?"

She turned, and there was a businessman with her duffel in his hands. "You left this in the bathroom," he said to her.

Her smile returned. "So I did," she said and took the duffel from him, reaching into the front pocket and pulling out the red cup holder. She grabbed the chai cup by the edges and placed it into the cup holder, then took the holder in her hands. "Thank you."

"Oh, no problem." And with that, the man grabbed his own coffee, as well as a small paper bag, and headed to the nearest wooden table.

She shouldered her bag and sat in the front of the cafe, on a stool, setting her bag below her feet. There was a huge window in front of her, the only such window in the cafe. Most everybody else liked to sit in the back, where the leather chairs and small chandeliers were, so they could carry on private conversations without being heard. But there was something special about this window. Here, she could sip her chai and watch the people of the city go by. This was one of her favorite parts of her day, because she loved people watching. There were eight million people in the city, and each and every one of their lives was on display.

She could see the subway entrance outside the window,

just across the street, and the crowds of people hurrying up and down the stairs, papers in hand. Women ran across the avenue with tennis shoes on, sacrificing style for comfort until they got to the office. Kids walked alongside the sidewalk in groups, headed to school to learn their numbers and letters. One woman walked by with three dog leashes in hand, and three different dogs pulling her in three different directions.

The world is full of possibility, she told herself. *You just have to know where to find it.*

She jumped and almost fell off of her chair when she heard a noise behind her. Turning, she saw that the noise had come from the same man in a suit who had retrieved her duffel for her. He was still seated over at a table in the other part of the café. It looked as if everything was fine, but --

With no warning, the man tried to grab for his throat and fell off his own chair, it clattering against the tile. This time, the sound startled everybody in the coffee shop. Bystanders got up from their chairs to help and to see what was going on, and even she was curious. What was the story here?

Getting off her own stool, she tried to get a better look as a woman screamed. The man was sprawled out on the ground, his coffee spilled everywhere, and the woman who had screamed was standing by his body with a look of utter horror on her face. A barista came up behind her, and she leaned on his arm, grateful for the support.

Most of the other patrons chose that moment to leave; she grabbed her duffel and ducked out just as the ambulance arrived. She walked out onto 72nd as a crowd continued to gather, shop patrons mixing with passersby. The lady who had screamed was talking with one of the medics as they strapped the man to a board and loaded him into the ambulance.

"You know, it's not going to matter what they do," a voice from behind her said. She turned around and saw an older woman sitting on the sidewalk with an apple in her hand. The woman's grey hair was done up in a bun, and she was wearing a red and green tracksuit. At first look, she seemed homeless.

Normally she did not associate with anybody like this -- mostly because she knew from previous experience that a lot of people who asked for money were scams. But there was something about the way she had just said that sentence that piqued her interest. She clutched her chai. "What do you mean?"

The old lady looked at her apple, not looking up at all as she spoke. "It's a waste of time, taking that man to the hospital. He's already dead."

Her brown eyes widened as she put her chai down. How did she know that? She didn't want to provoke her. "All he did was eat a bagel," she finally said.

The little old lady with the apple nodded. "Of course. All he did was eat a bagel." And, as if to drive home a point, she took a bite out of her apple.

That did it. She grabbed her duffel and, hanging on to her chai, hoofed it the rest of the way to school. Dead? Just like that? She would have to watch the news later that night...sounded like something that would be covered, even in a passing report. The sooner she got to school, the sooner she could finish her chai, the sooner she could forget about the creepy lady outside the Saint Arbucks.

But she couldn't forget.

2

Someday's Dreamer

She made it to school just in time to hear the National Anthem being played over the public address system. It was a bit old fashioned to do so, in her opinion, but it still gave a regular ritual to start the day with. She ran into the brick building's huge double doors and down the spacious halls, stopping at a locker and organizing herself. The duffel was emptied and she grabbed her math and biology books. She then stuffed her duffel in and closed and locked the locker, the red cup holder going with it.

Classroom 302 was her homeroom. From here, she would go to room 224 and take biology with Mrs. Anders, and then room 114 with Mr. Withrow for math. Now, though, she just had to make it through homeroom --

"Miss Lopez!"

She jumped; turning around in the hallway, she spotted the last person she had wanted to see this morning: Peter Doyle, the hall monitor and a mortal enemy of hers. His six foot tall, bulky football player frame filled the entire hallway.

"You're late," he said.

She rolled her eyes. "It's been a long morning --"

"No excuses." And with that, Peter took her by the shoulder, and she had no choice but to follow him to room 302.

The room turned quiet as she approached, and she could

hear Mrs. Bellemore starting the morning's announcements. She filed behind Peter as he knocked on the huge wooden door. Within seconds, Mrs. Bellemore answered.

"Miss Lopez," she said in that harsh voice that most every student had learned to fear. "You understand that this is the third time you have been late this month."

She took a deep breath. Actually, the first two tardies hadn't counted because her train had been late both times, and she had gotten proof. But she didn't have that as a buffer today. Instead, she told the truth. "A man collapsed at Saint Arbucks this morning," she said, loud enough for the entire class to hear. "I think he died."

The entire classroom was so still one could hear a pin drop. Peter moved away from the door and disappeared down the hall, presumably to harass other late students. Even Mrs. Bellemore looked stunned; she just opened the door and let her in.

"Hey, Carissa!"

She turned towards the back and identified Mark, the class clown. "Nice excuse!" he said, and there were scattered chuckles throughout the room.

Well. If they didn't believe she was telling the truth, she would just have to prove it. She walked to her desk, just right across from Mark's. "He was an older businessman," she told him, her voice soft but steady. "I left my duffel bag in the bathroom and he got it for me. Five minutes later, he was just eating his bagel when he fell over backwards." She turned towards the front and made eye contact with Mrs. Bellemore. "Can we start class now?"

Thankfully Mark shut up, and the rest of homeroom went well. The gossip spread like wildfire, though, and by the time Carissa got to room 224, it seemed like everybody in school knew about her Saint Arbucks adventure...if one could call it that.

"Are you serious?" her best friend Isabel asked her as they sat down next to each other and pulled out their biology books. "Dang, *chica*, that is some excuse."

"It's not an excuse. You would have been there too if you would have caught the one train on time. You always leave the house at the last possible second if I don't call you first."

"Whatever." Isabel looked up from her papers. "The point is that you actually made it to school...woah..." Her eyes became fixated on something. "Who's the new white kid?"

What? Carissa looked around the classroom until she saw who Isabel was talking about. The kid in question was new...er. She had definitely seen him before, but if she remembered correctly, he had been at this school since the beginning of this year. He was tall, with red hair and green eyes. At the moment, he was just sitting in the back of class with his nose in a book.

"He's not new," she finally said.

"Oh, really? He's not too bad looking actually, for a white guy. You know his name?"

Carissa thought about it for a minute and realized, no, she

didn't. She was saved by the fact that Mrs. Anders came into the room at that moment, and class began. She lost herself in facts and figures and life science. At one point, the teacher handed back graded papers in rows, and she got another glimpse of the boy in back with the red hair and the book. *Probably a total geek,* she thought to herself, and Isabel didn't typically go for those types.

She looked down at the papers, but none of them rang a bell as far as a name.

Biology ended and math was next, a class Carissa didn't have with Isabel. But she did have it with the nameless guy, who again sat in the back and kept reading his book without nearly any break in mode at all.

"And that's why both sides have to balance out," Mr. Withrow continued. "Just because you just came back from winter recess does not give you the excuse to sleep in class. That means you, Miss Harrigan."

Everybody turned and laughed as one girl in the back rose her head from her arms, guilty as charged. Mr. Withrow smiled. "Now, can anybody tell me the answer to problem 13?"

Carissa looked down at her own paper and shook her head. The problem with problem 13 was that it had required three different steps in order to finish it. The first two had been long and complicated enough, let alone the third step, which she had attempted four times over break.

The classroom sat silent for too long. Finally, Mr. Withrow

looked toward the back. "Mac?"

Without any warning, the boy with the book rose from his seat, putting the book itself on the desk, and walked up to the front of the classroom. Then, without saying a word, he picked up a piece of chalk and wrote out the entire solution on the blackboard, with no fanfare whatsoever. As he walked back to his seat, Carissa caught a glimpse of his face: while it wasn't traumatized, Mac certainly hadn't wanted to get up from his seat for some reason.

The rest of the day went on, uneventful for the most part. Since it was the first day back, some classes went easy on the students and some didn't. Carissa found herself with three pages of math homework already, problems much like the one Mac had done in class. She thought back to how Mr. Withrow had called on him. It was like Mr. Withrow knew that Mac could do the problem, like Mac was a last resort. How smart was this Mac person, anyway?

The train ride home was a simple affair, although Carissa almost got kicked by a couple of kids performing tricks on the subway. When she arrived home, she climbed up four floors of stairs to her apartment only to realize that, no, her mother was not home yet, and it was four floors back down to walk the neighbor's poodle.

Mama didn't do much after she finally did arrive home, other than sit down in front of the television and watch her novelas. Carissa put together her own dinner, knowing that her father would again be too late home to see her awake, and headed to her bedroom, pushing aside the beaded entry.

The room was full of posters, clothes lying around, a mostly unmade bed, and two closed closet doors that hid the rest of the mess. Carissa sat down her duffel, suddenly remembering the man who had returned it to her. Was he really dead? Or was that old lady as crazy as she seemed? And she did seem quite crazy.

Carissa opened up her computer and searched online, finding the news for New York. Certainly if something that crazy had happened in the early morning hours, it would still be somewhere on the page. Searchable, at least. But it wasn't. No matter how many news sites Carissa looked at, she couldn't find any reports of the incident ever happening.

Weird.

She slept on it, hoping that in the morning, this time it would make more sense. Her mother had the news on as she woke up and went into the kitchen to make her breakfast. She checked her smartphone and got a message from Isabel -- she had caught the express, so they would meet up at the same Saint Arbucks Carissa had been at the previous day.

"So he was just sitting here and he keeled back?" Isabel asked as she sipped her iced coffee.

Carissa was so glad to have her chai again this morning. "Yep," she said. "No warning at all. It just kind of happened."

"To be honest, I'm glad I wasn't here when it happened," Isabel said. "I would have probably freaked out."

"And they would have had to take you in an ambulance as well," Carissa noted.

"Ambulance?" one of the baristas asked. "When did this happen?"

Carissa gave a nervous chuckle. "Oh, it never happened with my friend here, but yesterday there was an ambulance here. Someone collapsed."

The barista gave Carissa a strange look. "There weren't any ambulances here yesterday. I was here all day. I would have had to sign off on the accident report."

"Hah!" Isabel said as Carissa struggled to make sense of it all. "So it was just a story to get you into class late!"

"It wasn't," Carissa said. She looked at the barista. "It was here, on 72nd and Broadway, around this time. A man fell out of his chair and someone called an ambulance. Oh -- and a woman screamed, really loudly. Everybody heard it."

"You've had too much chai," Isabel said. "Perhaps we need to get you to class..."

But Carissa wasn't paying attention to Isabel. For the crazy lady from yesterday was outside, eating another apple, looking straight at her.

3

Not The Only One

The next morning, Carissa found herself late for school again.

She didn't want to blame herself, but this time she couldn't cover with a fancy story. Not that yesterday had been a fancy story, mind you. She was certain that there had been an accident, that a man had really collapsed and possibly died at the Saint Arbucks on 72nd and Broadway.

Principal Digel wasn't fazed, though.

"I simply do not understand how you kids come up with these crazy excuses," the older woman told a shocked Carissa the next morning after her lateness (Mrs. Bellemore had sent her there upon her late arrival, much to Isabel's pleasure, though Carissa knew she could get her friend back later). "You dilly dally around at home playing your video games and what not and then you decide that somebody collapsed at the coffee shop. You are aware that we check all tardy alibi, Miss Lopez."

Carissa nodded. "I am aware."

"So you are also aware that I would find out about your ruse. Which spread quickly in the school hallways, I will also tell you."

One more nod from Carissa. "The problem is that I did actually see it happen. You know that I would not make up stories about why I'm late. For example, this morning, I was late. But it was my own fault, and I do accept responsibility. And if you do not believe me, you can check my file."

Principal Digel got up from her chair and reached behind her, where all of the student files were kept (in her office so they would not be stolen). She flipped through them until she found Lopez's name. "Let's see," she said as she flipped through Carissa's file...and the look on her face changed.

"Well," she said. "You have backed up every one of your tardies, except these most recent two. It does seem to be an anomaly." She put the file away. "Very well, Miss Lopez, but don't let it happen again." With that, Carissa was dismissed back to class.

It was true that Carissa couldn't back up her tardiness this morning -- it was completely due to the fact that she had had a horrible dream. A dream involving the creepy old lady from out front of Saint Arbucks, eating the apple she had been holding and staring at Carissa as if she had done something wrong.

It had been so terrifying that Carissa had rolled back over and went back to sleep in an effort to wipe the dream from her mind. Not only had that not worked, she had missed her train.

She walked herself back to class, hoping after the morning's events that the day could only get better. But it didn't. She couldn't forget the dream, no matter how hard she tried, and she almost fell asleep in her math class. When she got to the lunchroom for her meal, they were out of pizza, so she had to buy a peanut butter and jelly sandwich instead. Plus, Isabel was in a bad mood, and anytime Isabel was in a bad mood, so was Carissa by default.

"You can't be still talking about that dead guy thing," Isabel said as she ate a bite of her pizza. "Just give it a break already."

Carissa sighed. "That's the problem, Isabel. I just can't. I know I saw what I saw, and it's not like I can just unsee it."

"Well, maybe it was just a dream."

"Isabel, I know what was a dream, and it wasn't the guy collapsing in Saint Arbucks yesterday morning." Carissa shuddered. "Seriously, if I ever see that woman again, I am calling the cops."

"What woman?" Isabel realized, and Carissa knew then that her best friend had no idea what she was talking about. She sighed. She had to change the subject before Isabel gave her the runaround again.

"Oh, by the way," she said, to change the subject, "I found out who the guy you were looking at yesterday is. Turns out that he's some smart kid who can do a lot of math. Mr. Withrow seems to like him for some reason. Called him out by name, even -- oh, his name is Mac. I don't know if it's short for something or not. But there you go."

Isabel looked less than thrilled. "A geek? He knows how to

do math? Eww. I think I'll pass."

You're ridiculous, Carissa almost said, but she didn't want to hurt her best friend's feelings. They had been best friends for years, and Carissa knew better than to disagree with Isabel on the subject of a guy. So she let it go and spent the rest of her lunch break eating her sandwich and listening to Isabel rant on and on about reality television.

After lunch was English, a subject that Carissa couldn't care less about. Her favorite class, American History, was last in the day's schedule, and all she had to do was suffer through fifty minutes of who knew what. Then, she would be in history...nothing particularly special about it, but it did also signal the end of the day. At that point, she could go out with Isabel and the rest of her friends, maybe stop by the Burger Fender on the corner and grab a chicken sandwich for dinner.

As she sat in her seat, she realized that she had forgotten her English book. She checked the clock; she still had three minutes to make it there and back. In high school time, that was practically an eternity, especially if they were three minutes not in class. She got up from her chair and exited the room, walking at a brisk pace as she did so, curls bouncing.

Her locker was thankfully nearby, and she reached it and unlocked it. When she reached inside the locker to get her book, though, a small white piece of paper fell out and onto the ground. Carissa pursed her lips and bent down to pick it up.

"You saw it too, didn't you? The man in the Saint Arbucks who collapsed all of a sudden?"

She gasped and almost dropped the note -- this note had obviously been left for her. Steadying herself on the locker door, she took another look at the note. It had been typed, which only added to its mystery. Whoever this was who sent the note didn't want to be revealed just yet.

"You don't know who I am yet. And that's okay. Because I don't know you yet either. All I know is that we both saw the same thing yesterday morning, and nobody else will back up our claim. If you're not scared, you can meet me on the roof after school. I'll be waiting there if you want to discuss this further. I don't have answers, but at least now you know you're not crazy." There was one final note at the bottom. *"Also, I know you saw what I saw because you announced it to your entire homeroom class, Word spreads fast."*

Carissa did her best job to stay calm and failed. Who was this person? How had they known where her locker was? She took a deep breath, then stuffed the note in the front of her English book and sprinted down the hallway, just making it to class on time.

Wednesdays were usually spent hanging out with friends after school, but on this January 9th, Carissa clearly had different plans. She grabbed her white duffel from her locker and her red coat as well, and was about to leave when she heard a familiar voice.

"Haaaaaay *chica*, so are we going out or what?"

Carissa had to think of a plan and fast. She didn't want to lie to her best friend -- even a bit -- but if she heard one more thing about the Saint Arbucks incident that wasn't (according to her), she would lose her mind. "I can't today," she said. "Busy." Which was all true, at this point.

"Busy with what?" Oh, Carissa knew that Isabel was going to ask that question.

"My mom wants me home early," she said. And that was actually true. Her dad was off of work tonight, and her mother had wanted to have a nice dinner with the three of them together. It would just have to happen after Carissa found out who sent the note to her locker.

Isabel sighed. "Fine. But you owe me." With that, she turned around and set off in the opposite direction, probably to go meet up with some other friends.

Carissa relished in her new found freedom -- for five whole minutes. Then, she headed towards the roof. Usually students weren't allowed on the roof, and her track record this week on office visits was not going well. But if this person had answers, then she was going to go and at least investigate.

She remembered where the stairs were; she walked back up to the fourth floor, which only had freshman classes on it, and down all the way to the end of the hallway. There was a huge sign there saying that only police were allowed on the roof, and any student caught up there would be suspended. Normally Carissa adhered to rules, but this time, she just had to be proven right.

She stepped past the sign and checked to see if anybody was around. Nope. Everybody had already left for the day. With that, she skipped up the back set of stairs to the door. This door was an emergency exit, but the door was cracked open, and there were no sirens, which meant it was safe to touch. Carissa pushed it.

The roof was huge, expansive, without much of a view and with too many pigeons. Somebody was up there already, standing among the pigeons. When Carissa got a closer look, she gasped. She would know that hair anywhere, even if the person wasn't looking at her.

It was Mac.

4

Up On The Roof

She couldn't believe it. But it was true. She had just been talking about him, and he was up here on the roof. Waiting for her. Probably. It could be possible that Mac was up on the roof for other reasons.

But then he turned from where he had been sitting near the pigeons, and Carissa knew: he was here for her. As he walked, the pigeons became startled and flew up into the air around the two of them.

"I wasn't sure if you would come or not," he said, and Carissa felt her nerves intensify.

"Well, I'm here. Why did you pick the roof to meet?"

"To be honest? Because I knew we wouldn't be followed up here. I'm the only student that I know of with a key to the roof. Mr. Withrow got me one after I asked him."

Carissa took a deep breath. It was certainly unsettling to be on the roof with a guy like this. Time to get down to business. "You said in your note that you had witnessed the accident at Saint Arbucks on Monday. You and I are apparently the only people who saw that."

Mac nodded, still a comfortable distance away from Carissa. "That's true. And to be honest, I don't know why. It would make sense that everybody would remember something like that, but they don't."

"Were you in the Saint Arbucks when it happened?"

"Actually, no, but I was just getting off the train at 72nd Street and I saw the ambulances there. When the rumor started going around school, I knew that was what I had seen."

Carissa nodded, then remembered one fact that Mac had left out. "Do you remember anything else?"

"No...why?"

It seemed important enough to mention. "There was this creepy old lady there, outside Saint Arbucks that morning. I think she was homeless. Said the guy who collapsed was dead. I saw her again yesterday but didn't talk to her." And then she added, "Mostly because she creeped me out."

"Sounds like it," Mac said, now standing near Carissa. He was a good three or four inches taller than her, plus or minus the hair that stuck up and defied gravity. "I'm sorry if it was weird to call you on the roof like this," he said, "but I couldn't think of another place where we could meet. I'm not sure we've ever properly met."

"You're Mac, right? I've seen you in class before. I'm Carissa Lopez." Carissa stuck out her hand, and Mac shook it with a smile on his face.

"My pleasure," he said. "Now seriously...why wouldn't anybody have seen what happened other than us two and that lady you mentioned?"

Carissa shrugged as she leaned against the door that led back down to the school's hallways. While the school did have four floors, it was mostly condensed on one address and was surrounded by taller buildings. That meant that some office workers in a skyscraper nearby could be spying on Carissa for all she knew. She wasn't nervous...mostly because nothing had happened of note on this roof. Yet. "When I went to the Saint Arbucks yesterday morning with Isabel for my chai," she said, "the barista overheard me talking about yesterday's events and said that I was lying, or that I had the wrong location. But I always go to that same Saint Arbucks, most every morning. Four out of five, at least." She grinned. "Gotta have my chai."

Mac laughed, and Carissa noticed how carefree he seemed. "I understand. I'm not a coffee drinker, but I do have my own vices."

She found herself interested, although she didn't know exactly why. "Like?"

He laughed again, but this time Carissa noticed that it was definitely more nervous. "Like coming to the roof, among other things. But I also have a soft spot for science fiction television. Can't miss an episode or I start showing signs of withdrawal."

Now Carissa had to laugh -- she knew what withdrawal felt like. "You don't talk a lot in class."

Mac's blush was evident as day on his pale skin. "I don't like to," he said. "Personal reasons."

"Oh." And Carissa left that at that. "So about this accident...how do we go about proving it to everybody?"

"To be honest, I'm not even sure we should," Mac told her. "It's not a huge deal to anyone except for us, because we know we saw it. I say we don't mention this around school anymore, which was another reason why I had us meet on the roof."

"That's true," Carissa said out loud. "My best friend is already telling me to shut up about the entire thing."

"But that's just it." Mac ran both of his hands through his red hair, white starched polo rising as he did so. "We can't even bother telling anybody else because they are so convinced that we are lying. What we have to do is find some way to first reprove to us that this happened. I think that the fact that someone died is less important than the fact that nobody remembers he died. Because if nobody remembers, then did he die in the first place?" He shrugged. "It's kind of like that 'if a tree falls in an empty forest' kind of thing. Do you know what I'm talking about?"

Carissa nodded. "You mean where if a tree falls and nobody hears it, did it still fall."

"Yeah. That type of thing. People die in many different ways every day here in the city. The difference here is that nobody believes it except for us."

Carissa thought about it for a moment. All of this was true. *And to think it all started with just an ordinary morning at Saint Arbucks,* she thought to herself. "So," she asked Mac, "you're the one who called me here. What is our next step?"

Then, without any warning, the door behind Carissa opened up, and two guards came out onto the roof. Behind them was Peter, with his usual smug look on his face.

"Well, well, well, look at what we have here," he said. "A couple of lovebirds on the roof."

Carissa felt her face flush -- Peter was so wrong, she didn't even properly know this Mac guy yet! Besides --

"In case you're wondering," Mac said, not fazed by Peter's appearance at all, "Mr. Withrow gave me a key to the roof back last semester when I was spray painting bottle rockets for class. He then said that I could come up here for anything, at any time. You'll have to take this up with him before you get the final say on any of this."

"You really honestly believe that a teacher would give you a roof key?" Peter asked. "It's against the school rules for anybody to be up here. Including teachers. And stuck up seniors like you."

Carissa made a mental note to ask Mr. Withrow about the roof tomorrow when she got to class. "You're on the roof now as well, in case you didn't notice," she said.

Peter realized his goof. "Guards, bring both of them downstairs to Principal Digel's office," he said. "I'm excited to hear the rumors that will spread at this school about the two of you on the roof. There better not be any trash left up here when you leave...if you know what I mean."

Eww. Carissa couldn't even begin to wonder how disgusting the entire situation was.

Before she could react, however, Mac did. He grabbed her by the arm and pulled her to one side. Carissa hadn't realized how strong he was – she grabbed her duffel and followed him as he started running toward the edge of the roof.

And then she realized where she was going. "Mac --"

He jumped off of the roof, and she went with him. They fell a grand total of three feet -- onto the cramped fire escape of the building next to the school. Mac let go of Carissa as she steadied herself on the escape, grabbing onto the railing. Her own apartment building had one of these, but she had never been allowed on one.

"Careful," Mac said as he grabbed a hold of the structure as well. Then, he started to go down the stairs. "Hold on tight."

"Um, okay," Carissa said as she followed behind him, white duffel now in tow. They went down two flights of shaky fire escape stairs until they got to the second floor. The ladder used to descend from here was already unlocked.

"I use this all the time," Mac explained as he lowered the ladder. "You look like you have never been on one of these things before."

"You would be right," Carissa said, her nerves showing. She then realized that something odd was missing. "Didn't you bring a coat?"

"I'll get it tomorrow." Mac practically flew down the ladder. "We need to get away from those guys as soon as possible. They'll know that we're down here now, and if we take any longer, they'll get to us."

Carissa nodded and forced herself to get over the fear of heights she now had. She took a deep breath, shouldered her duffel, and slowly descended the stairs. When she reached the bottom, Mac was waiting there for her.

"There we go," he said. "And we're lucky enough that the guards and Peter aren't here yet."

"Where do we go next?" Carissa said.

"Well, you could always go back to your apartment," Mac said. "Or you can join me in running away from these guys. I need to get back in Brooklyn before they know I'm here."

Wait -- what? "You're from Brooklyn? What are you doing in school all the way up here on the Upper West Side? That's got to be some commute --"

"Too late." Mac grabbed Carissa by the arm. "You're going to have to trust me. They're at the front gate of the school. We need to run. Now."

Carissa nodded, although she wasn't sure why -- did she trust this guy? And then she spotted Peter, the last person she wanted to see at that moment, looking left and right for them.

"Okay," she said. "But you're paying for my subway fare."

Mac laughed. "I won't need to."

5

Checking Facts

"What do you mean, we're not taking the subway?" But Carissa's voice was drowned out by the hustle and bustle as Mac continued to lead her on, through the alleyway between their escape building and the school. It deposited them neatly on 71st.

"This way," Mac said, and as before, he didn't wait for Carissa to stop and give the okay to move on. Instead, they just did.

I have got to have a discussion with you when this is all said and done, Carissa thought to herself. *And there better be a Saint Arbucks chai involved.*

They ran down the street, Mac looking over his shoulder every once in a while to see if anybody was following them. So far, they were in the clear, but Carissa remembered the look on Peter's face when he had found the two of them on the roof...not to mention some of the things he had said. She closed her eyes and kept running.

They reached the street corner and Carissa looked up, curious to know exactly where they were. "So what is --"

"Here." Mac ducked under another, different fire escape, and Carissa found herself back in another alleyway with a trash can and -- it suddenly made sense.

"We're going to bike all the way to Brooklyn?" she asked

as Mac unlocked the ordinary looking bicycle from where it had been locked against the fire escape. "And why do you keep it locked up here? They have bike racks at school, you know."

"Oh, I know," Mac said with a smile. He motioned to the bike. "You'll have to put your feet on those rungs there and hold onto my shoulders." Carissa checked and, sure enough, there were small ledges where she could put her feet. Mac straddled the bike, and she strapped her duffel securely against her back, then put her feet up on the ledges and grabbed Mac's shoulders.

"You have to promise me you're not going to let go," Mac said as he jumped up onto the bike seat and started to pedal down the alleyway.

"Why would I let go?" Carissa asked.

And then, without any warning, the bicycle started to fly down the street, at a faster speed than Carissa had been anticipating. She gripped Mac's shoulders tighter as he swerved onto Amsterdam Avenue. "We'll stay on Amsterdam until we hit Columbus Circle, and then we gotta go to the East Side," Mac yelled.

Carissa realized why he was yelling -- he had to yell to be heard over the motor sound she could now identify. "You have a motorbike?"

"It's an e-bike. There's a difference. Gas bikes are illegal, but electric ones aren't. Not yet, anyway." Mac looked back and grinned at her. "I can control it up here, by my brakes. Let me know if I start going too fast."

Carissa nodded, finally understanding how someone could come from Brooklyn to Manhattan for school every day.

They made their way onto the main drag, and Mac parked in front of a very familiar looking Saint Arbucks. "Why are we stopping here?" Carissa asked. She scanned the area quickly, but there was no sign of the creepy lady so far.

"Going inside to check my facts. I'd like to know if any of the baristas would show me the accident report for an accident that doesn't exist. Do you have a pen and a pad of paper? I clearly don't have any of that on me." That was true: Carissa now noticed that Mac didn't have a backpack on him. Maybe he didn't need one.

"Good idea," she said as she whipped around her duffel and started looking for her pencil case. "We should work quickly, though, so Peter and his friends don't catch up to us..." Her voice trailed off.

Mac noticed the concerned look on her face. "What's wrong?"

Carissa showed him the picture that she had found in her bag. "It was just sitting in there. I cleaned the entire thing out yesterday, so..."

Mac took a closer look. "It's a photograph. Didn't think that they still printed them like this. I mean, I know they can do that at certain Bleecker Liz drugstores, but --"

"No, look," Carissa said as she pointed at the man and the woman in the picture. "That man -- he was the one who collapsed here on Monday." The photo was older, but Carissa remembered his face well. He was younger than he had been on Monday, which probably dated this photo by at least a decade...especially if this glossy photo had been developed and not only printed from a file. It was him, though, that blonde hair and big smile. But the woman who was in the photo also looked familiar, and Carissa finally realized why. "Her," she said. "The lady."

Mac looked confused. "What?"

"The lady in the picture -- did I tell you about the homeless lady who was sitting outside the Saint Arbucks on Monday? She said the guy who collapsed died? It's the eyes. Her hair in this picture is brown, but she has the same piercing blue eyes. It has to be her."

When Carissa looked up from the photo, she saw her worst nightmare in recent memory come true: a police officer was standing near their Saint Arbucks, talking to the same old lady. She was wearing the same clothes and same red and green tracksuit she had always worn, which furthered Carissa's assumption that she might be homeless.

But then the lady looked away from the red apple she was holding and the policeman who was talking to her and she looked straight at Carissa with those eyes. At the same time, the policeman followed the woman's gaze, but his eyes landed on

Mac instead.

"Get back on the bike," he whispered just as the policeman started running for them.

Carissa tried not to think of every Spanish curse word her mama used when she was mad. In shock, she zipped up her bag and jumped on just as Mac started up the bike again, and they were off. She gripped his shoulders for dear life, glad she was at least getting away from that creepy lady again...but what was with that cop?

They zoomed down towards 59th Street, and Mac took a left, slowing down a bit as he passed the packed roadways, zipping between cars as if he was born to do this. Carissa could only hold on for dear life and pray they did not wreck – she was used to traveling underground, not by bike, much less a powered bike. They finally turned right when Mac reached Second Avenue, and Mac sped up the bike.

"Stay calm," he said as they dove right into a construction site. The new subway line was being built right below them, and they had to dodge not only cars but trucks and construction vehicles while going south. Carissa suddenly felt as if she was part of a chase in some thriller movie. The next thing she knew, there would be cop cars surrounding her, probably to interrogate her about the accident on Monday. But then Mac would ride up a ramp and jump in midair, and everything would go into slow motion, and there would probably be a close up on Carissa's shocked face.

But there were no police cars, and the pair made it all the way through the Upper East Side, slowing down at 60th to avoid all of the cars taking the Queensboro Bridge out of Manhattan, then through Murray Hill. Carissa looked at a display clock in Union Square and saw that they had made great time on this bike -- almost as fast as the subway, without all of the restraints of a hard line system. They then went down past Houston Street and into Chinatown. Carissa felt the bike slow as Mac turned onto the Brooklyn Bridge.

"I'm not going to take you all the way to my neighborhood," Mac explained. "That would be too far, I think. Where do you live again?"

"The Heights. My family has had the same apartment for years."

"Then we'll stop downtown here, check in with someone I know, and then we'll get you on a train back home. Sound good?"

"Yeah. Where are you from, anyway?"

"All the way down in Coney Island. Yeah, I know it's far, but I don't mind."

Especially with a motorized bike like this one, Carissa noted.

She held on tight as Mac turned off the electric component to the bike, then pedaled up to the ramp. "Hey," she said, now that she could talk and her voice wasn't being drowned out, "what's up with that police officer? You know, you were all like 'get back on the bike' but you didn't give any reasons."

"Let's just say me and that cop are not friends," Mac said. "At all."

Carissa looked around herself and noticed that they were actually on the bridge now. She looked behind herself and saw the skyline of Manhattan rise behind her as the bike went on. It wasn't very often that she got this view of her hometown, the city she had lived in for all of her seventeen years. One could consider Manhattan a bubble if they went too long without seeing this view.

"Nice, huh?" Mac said.

"You know I'm looking at the city?"

"Yeah -- I have a rear view mirror." Mac laughed. "I assume you don't see it like this often?"

He had read her mind -- not literally, although that would not surprise her given the recent turn of events. "So where are we heading again?"

"Just off Borough Hall. I have a friend who works at a little place there called Kofenya. It's a real hipster joint, but I can score you a free chai."

Carissa grinned. "Sold. But why there specifically?"

"Because this friend of mine knows a thing or two about cameras. He's a professional photographer, and the best friend of my boss when he was a kid. He'll be able to take one look at that

41

photo and tell us all sorts of useful information -- well, about the photo anyway. Can't tell us about the people."

Carissa was about to ask about Mac's supposed job, but he increased his pedaling speed, and the question was lost to the wind as they rode towards Brooklyn.

6

Kofenya

Borough Hall was busy at this time of day; it seemed like everybody was going everywhere at once. The atmosphere was not as rushed as Manhattan had been, but the crowds still went along at a nice pace.

Mac had to keep the bike motor off the entire way into Brooklyn. "Have you been here before?" he asked Carissa.

The girl was still holding on tight for dear life. "I have," she said. "It's just been a while. I think the last time my class was in downtown Brooklyn was when we had to come to the Transit Museum for a science field trip. And I don't know how many years ago that was."

"Oh." Mac gave her a smile. "You'll like this place that I'm taking you to."

They passed by the huge Borough Hall building, then through some commercial areas until they were on a back street. Kofenya was on the corner, what appeared to be a small joint with a simple sign over the door. Mac parked his bike outside and chained it to the nearest light post.

"Come on in," he said with a smile again. "They won't bite at all."

It's not the people in the coffee joint that I'm afraid of, Carissa thought to herself. But she didn't want to tell Mac that.

Here he was, a strange boy who was also caught in this crossfire just as she had been. But something wasn't adding up for her. How did Mac have a key to the roof? Where did he get his cool bike? And why was that cop going straight for him at the Saint Arbucks? There were so many questions and Carissa felt like she couldn't properly trust Mac until she got some of them answered.

But then again...he had gotten her here to Brooklyn in one piece. And he had also seen the accident. He was the proof that Carissa herself was not crazy. She took a deep breath, straightened the bag on her back, and then walked towards the door, opening it and searching for Mac.

Kofenya looked like any regular indie cafe in Brooklyn. Carissa had figured that the plush seats would be filled with hipsters who would be taking in the artwork on the walls, but there weren't a lot of people there at this time of day. There were two friends talking in a corner over some textbooks, a boy in a corner with a book that was clearly too big to be anything but a Bible and a pad of paper, and another boy with a computer.

For a place here near Borough Hall, Carissa thought to herself, *they sure don't get a lot of foot traffic.* She shrugged and went up to the counter. The barista was a short, skinny girl with tightly curled long black hair and an infectious smile on her face.

"Welcome to Kofenya!" she said. "What can I get for you?"

Carissa grinned. "I'd like a chai and...one of those

44

chocolate brownies," she said. And then she pointed at Mac. "Oh, and he's paying."

Mac, who had been sitting in the corner looking over a menu (Carissa wasn't sure why, as the entire drink menu at least was listed up on the wall) looked up at the mention of his name. "What now?" he asked.

"Oh, come on. You were the one who brought me all the way to Brooklyn to meet this person who works here. You're definitely covering the tab on this one." Carissa smiled. "But if the chai is good enough and I come back, I'll pay then."

Mac rolled his eyes. "Oh, trust me, you'll be back."

It didn't take Carissa two seconds after receiving her chai to know that Mac was right. This chai was amazing -- maybe even more so than the chai that she usually got at Saint Arbucks every morning before school. She grinned. "So is this the other reason that you live in Brooklyn?"

"No," Mac said. "Me living in Brooklyn has nothing to do with being in the same borough as this store. Although it certainly helps. Hey, Dan!"

Carissa looked at where Mac was looking and saw a tall, almost geeky looking kid with dark hair and glasses on coming out of the back room. "This is Dan," Mac explained to Carissa. "He's my friend I told you about, the one who knows everything about cameras. Long time no see," he said as he bumped fists with Dan.

Dan just smiled; Carissa took him as the type of person who would rather spend their time with their electronics than actual people. But still, he was here, and he did give her a smile, albeit small. "Good afternoon, Mac! And who is your new girlfriend?"

Carissa was mid sip and had to avoid swallowing it the wrong way. She felt her face light up like the fourth of July. "We're not dating," she said, suddenly unable to look Mac in the eye. She didn't even know this kid and yet he had driven her all the way to his home borough. No wonder random people who didn't know any better already thought there was more there than there was. It was because she already trusted Mac -- more than she probably should, as well.

"Carissa is a friend from school," Mac explained. "She found a picture in her duffel earlier today, and we were wondering if we could get some stats out of it. You know, what camera it was taken with and what not." When he said 'what not,' Carissa noted that Mac's voice seemed to have a slight accent to it, though she didn't know the origin of it, and it was gone before she could think about it too much.

"Got it." Dan smiled at Carissa. "Let me see it."

They all sat around a table in the corner of the cafe, on what appeared to be old theater seats. Carissa sat next to Mac and blushed at their close proximity when she put her duffel on the table. *Chill out, Carissa,* she told herself. *You're just thinking stupid stuff because you've spent a lot of time with him today. Breathe.*

She then took out the picture. "This is it," she said.

Dan took the photo from her and looked it over. "Well, it was a 35 millimeter camera, that's for sure," he said. "I can tell just from the exposure." When he turned the picture, Carissa saw a medium sized smudge on the back, along with a silver logo that she had never seen before.

"What's that?" she asked.

Dan flipped the photo over. "I don't know what the smudge is from," he said. "But this X logo is from Piñeiro -- they're a film company that went out of business a few years back. They never made the transition to digital. I'd at least say this picture was taken before the new millennium." He flipped the picture over so Mac and Carissa could see the man, now dead, and the creepy lady in their glory, minus a few years according to Dan.

"It's surreal," Carissa said.

"Any clue as to the camera?" Mac asked.

Dan took a closer look at the photo. "Just looks like a regular -- wait. The edges are a bit rounded. I can't believe I missed that before! So yeah, it's got to be a LaPostale model, I'd say one of their Bright 2500 models or older, but not before 1200. That's when they started doing these rounded edges. They did that for years until they switched over to digital. It was their trademark in the film world."

"LaPostale is that one company that makes everything, right?" Carissa asked for clarification.

Mac nodded. "They made the motor to my bike. Thanks for the information, Dan. Carissa, do you want a refill on your chai?"

The two of them sat in the cafe for a while -- almost like a date, though Mac kept an excellent distance from her the entire time -- and gave more in depth introductions to their world. Carissa was a third generation Hispanic in the Heights; he was being raised by his mom in Coney Island. "My mom emigrated, too, from Ireland," Mac explained. "My full name is Macardle Irving Taggart -- you can see why I go by Mac."

She giggled. "That would certainly make your life much easier."

Mac nodded, almost staring off into space. "I'm sorry that I had to drag you all the way to Brooklyn to find this information out. With this, at least we know it was definitely those two at a younger age."

"But who is the man, and who really is the woman? And how did that picture end up in my bag in the first place? That's what I would like to know." Carissa finished off her chai. "It's been a long day. What train do I need to take from here to get home? I'm surprised my mama hasn't called already to see where I am." She reached into her pocket and pulled out her phone; sure enough, no missed calls. "Hmm." She unlocked it and dialed her home number, waiting. "Mama should be home by now. Why isn't she picking up?"

"Maybe she got kidnapped by aliens." That was Dan, who had stopped by to take Carissa's empty chai mug. "And she's being held hostage until she gives them the music box they're looking for."

"Dan, that's a movie plot," Mac said with another roll of his eyes. "Quit being fantastic."

"Guys, seriously," Carissa said as she rang her home phone again. "My mama never doesn't pick up. I'm starting to get worried that something's wrong."

Mac got up from the table. "I'll take you."

"You don't have to --"

Mac looked Carissa in the eyes. "Oh, trust me. I do."

7

Crookery and Churros

They easily made it back to Manhattan without any problems; the rush hour crowds had tapered off considerably. Mac was able to get away with keeping his motor running consistently, which meant that Carissa got a face full of cold wind as the skyscrapers loomed above her.

Without Carissa even needing to say, Mac took the same route he had before: up First Avenue this time, then across Harlem to Amsterdam. "Where exactly do you live?" he asked at this point.

"181st and Saint Nick. Do you know this area?"

He laughed again. "You don't want to know how I know this area." And so the enigma of Mac continued. Carissa wished he would just tell her something.

The apartment windows looked dark when Carissa got there -- not good, she footnoted to herself. She got off of the bike as Mac slowed it down for her. "Are you okay?" he asked.

"I'll be better when I'm inside," Carissa said as she took out her keys from the coat pocket she kept them in. Without thinking of any of the danger she could be putting herself in, she unlocked the front door and ran up the stairs, not even bothering to wait for Mac.

"Mama?" she asked as soon as she unlocked the front door

and turned on the lights. "Where are you? You should be home by now." She considered to herself that she should have checked the hair salon first to see if her mother had gotten held up by a customer -- that happened on occasion. But she always called even if that was the case. Having no contact from her mother made Carissa think that maybe she slipped and fell on something. For a split second, she wished she had remembered to let Mac into the apartment as well --

She heard something back in the bedroom. Going to the kitchen first, she grabbed a frying pan from the rack and held it close to her as a weapon. Then, she went into the back hallway to where the two bedrooms were and flipped on the light.

"Get out now!" she yelled as loudly as she could in Spanish.

The mysterious person was in the hall closet, but when he turned around, Carissa could see that he wasn't so mysterious anymore. "Peter?!?" she asked, still holding the frying pan. This had to be some sort of a dream. Perhaps Mac had crashed on his bike and she was unconscious. Either way, how was Peter from school in her apartment, without a key, looking around in her hall closet?

Peter turned to Carissa. "You're home."

Carissa bit her tongue, trying to prevent from using all the words that her mother told her not to use. "What are you doing here?"

"This." And Peter handed Carissa a pink slip of paper.

Carissa looked down at it and recognized the familiar handwriting of Principal Digel. "Detention? You came all the way here and broke into my house to give me a detention? Why can't you just leave me alone? I already told you that Mac had a key that a teacher gave him. And where's my mama?"

"Do me a favor and give this to your new boyfriend when you see him next," Peter said, handing Carissa another piece of pink paper with Mac's name on it. When she looked down at it, she saw scribbled "Theft and trespassing" as the reasons for the detention.

"Theft?" she asked.

"You know. Because he stole Mr. Withrow's key."

"He did no such thing. He told me that he got it from Mr. Withrow, yes, but it was not stolen. You're getting all your facts way wrong."

Peter shook his head. "It's you who is getting her facts wrong." With that, he took something out of his pocket and popped it into his mouth.

Carissa recognized that crunch anywhere. "Are those my mama's churros?!"

"So what if they are?"

Oh, if Carissa was mad before, she was livid now. But before she could do anything about it, Peter went cross eyed, then collapsed to the ground. Mac was standing right behind him, arm outstretched. "Talk about an invasion of personal space," he said.

"Invasion of personal space? You think this is an invasion of personal space? This is more than an invasion of personal space. This is madness!" Carissa felt like throwing something, but couldn't find anything to throw. "How did you get up here, anyway?"

"The fire escape. It was unlocked. I think that's how Peter got up here in the first place. What was he doing, anyway?" With that, Carissa handed Mac the detention slip, and he read it over, then laughed. "Theft? Seriously? I'll get this all settled in the morning. Not sure if it will invalidate our detentions, but at least we won't be bothered by Peter anymore. Is your mom here?"

"Carissa?" At that moment, her mother walked through the still open door to the apartment. "What is going on here?" she asked in Spanish, clearly in shock.

They ended up calling the police to escort Peter out, once he woke up. Thankfully Carissa explained what she could to the cops, and Peter got off with only a warning, but if he was ever sighted on the premises again he would be thrown in jail for at least the night. Carissa then had to explain to her mama where the churros went.

Her mama looked over at Mac, who was still looking at the pink detention slip as if it were something foreign. "Is that your new boyfriend?" she asked.

Seriously, Mama? You too? Carissa wanted to ask. But she

bit her tongue -- too long for her mama to stop from assuming. She simply clicked her tongue and said, "You always go for the white boys," and then went into her bedroom.

Carissa sighed. "I didn't do anything," she said as Mac walked back over to her.

"I'm sorry for all of this mess tonight," Mac said. He gave her a small smile. "I was hoping that someday we could meet under better circumstances. Perhaps I will see you sometime tomorrow at school?"

"You're headed all the way home tonight?" Carissa asked. This would be the fourth time he would go between boroughs this same day.

Mac nodded. "It's not like I can stay here, especially since I haven't received any invitation to do so. So, in the morning?"

Carissa nodded, and Mac left the way he had come -- by the fire escape. She watched him ride off in the dark and found herself wishing he would get back to Brooklyn okay.

She got ready for bed, knowing that the next day would be a busy one, but could not go to sleep for some reason. She stayed awake until the wee hours of the morning, finally giving in to exhaustion and waking up just on time. She threw her pink detention paper in her bag and ran out of the apartment to catch her train as her mother was making more churros.

She easily got to the train station. The countdown clock didn't say one was coming for at least ten more minutes -- odd in itself at this hour, maybe there was a problem at the terminal -- but a train did roll up. It was one of the new ones with shiny new floors, automated announcements, and detailed line maps. Carissa didn't think they were running special trains like this one on the 1 line, but she still got on. The doors closed behind her just as she realized she was the only one on the train.

She sat down as the train continued its journey -- but then sped right on through 168th Street's station without stopping. And 157th. And 145th. By the time the train skipped the elevated 125th Street station, Carissa was beginning to get spooked. What was the deal with this train?

"You do not understand, do you?"

Carissa jumped a mile -- she looked to her left and saw Mrs. Creepy Lady, sitting there with yet another apple, this one bright red in color as the others had been. "Stop scaring me like that!" Carissa said, now confident she was dreaming.

The lady smiled at Carissa as the train skipped 116th. "You won't stop and put the pieces together, will you? Carissa Lopez."

"This is starting to really freak me out," Carissa said as she moved to the other side of the car, making a motion to open the door that would lead to the next car. But it was locked. Go figure. She turned back to the lady. "I don't get this."

The car stayed silent as the lady continued to sit on the car bench, taking another bite out of her apple. "Tell me, what train are we on right now?"

Carissa had to look at the display to remind herself. "The 1 train."

"Ahh, yes. But are we really?"

Carissa sighed. "I don't know. It hasn't been stopping." And there, it did a fly by right through 96th Street. Carissa hoped that the people on the platform weren't standing too close to the yellow line.

"So there you go. Is it fact or fiction? You are the one who has the gift to discern, Carissa Lopez. And you must discern, before the fated day, before all is lost."

Carissa gripped her bag. "Fated day? Okay, you've lost me."

"Don't forget. The herald will bring you the information you seek, but the discernment must be only yours." The lady smiled as the lights flickered, and then the car's brakes engaged. Carissa reached for a bar and she found herself standing close to many other people. In fact, now she was on a regular 1 train again, with faded walls and announcements nobody could hear, crowded with people.

Weird, Carissa thought to herself. For the umpteenth time that week, she considered that maybe she had been dreaming something. With a sigh, she got off the train at 72nd Street as she always did. She looked back and saw the old train leave the station -- and the old lady, now standing on the old train, taking another bite out of the apple.

She felt the breath leave her body. "I gotta tell Mac."

8

Detention

"I'm serious, Carissa," Isabel said as she tapped her pencil against the desk for what seemed to be the millionth time. "You have got to stop making up these ridiculous stories."

Carissa rolled her eyes. "They're not just stories," she said. She should have known better than to tell practical Isabel about the bike ride to Brooklyn, or the fact that Peter was in her house yesterday by way of fire escape, or the strange train ride down to school that she wasn't even sure was real or not. But Carissa didn't have anybody else to tell these things to yet; after all, it was only the first class of the day, and she hadn't seen Mac yet. Not that she hadn't been looking; quite the opposite, in fact. She had almost been late to her first class because she had been looking down the halls for him, sticking mostly to her classroom hallway but curious nonetheless.

"They all sound like stories to me. Where is this Mac kid anyway? If he was in on this entire thing, I'd like to hear his side of the story."

"Isabel, I already told you, I haven't seen him yet today. When I see him, I'll make sure that he comes over to our table at lunch and explains everything to you."

"At our table? Seriously? You wouldn't expect a total geek like him to be welcome at our table."

"Except he's the total geek who has the answers you're looking for."

Isabel sighed. "You're right...I suppose." She took another big gulp out of her huge Saint Arbucks latte to go. "But he's only going to stop by. No staying."

"Isabel, he's being invited to the table. I think he can sit for one day."

Now it was Isabel's turn to roll her eyes. "If you like this white guy so much, then why don't the two of you just get together?"

Carissa was about to complain again that there was nothing between her and Mac, but Mrs. Bellemore chose that moment to start homeroom.

The day passed slowly until Carissa could finally get to Mr. Withrow's class. She was hoping to get some of her questions straightened out. But the longer she sat in her chair, the more apparent it was becoming that Mac wasn't showing up to class. She bit her tongue all the way through math, then went up to Mr. Withrow's desk after class was done.

"Do you know if Mac is on the absence list this morning?" she asked.

Mr. Withrow took out a sheet of paper and looked it over. "Taggart, Taggart...ahh, yes, there it is. His mother called it in this morning." Carissa silently hoped that nothing bad had happened to Mac, and that he was just recovering after a long day yesterday.

She herself was wishing she could take a day off to recover; she wasn't used to this much...spontaneity.

She tried to remember what the lady had said on the train that morning. Something about being prepared for something and asking a lot of questions. She couldn't remember it all at this point...and with it being the creepy lady, she wasn't sure she wanted to. Perhaps that was just another one of her dreams.

Her next order of business was to go to the office right before lunch. She would be a couple of minutes behind to her table -- something that Isabel was sure to complain about -- but she had to check the legality of this.

"I want to make sure that this is real," she said as she handed the pink detention slip over to the secretary. With Peter being the one who delivered it, she wanted to make sure it was actually real.

The secretary looked over the paper. "Were you on the roof?"

"Well, yeah --"

"Then it's real."

"I mean -- you know how when a detention slip is written there's a copy made of it? It's public knowledge."

The secretary sighed; Carissa could tell she was just so excited to be at work today. She reached behind her and found the book of records, flipping through it. "What's the date on the pink slip?"

"Yesterday -- the 9th."

"Mmhmm...I don't actually see it here, so I'll have to add it." And sure enough, when Carissa looked over at the list, she didn't see either her name or Mac's. She footnoted to herself that when she saw Mac next, she should tell him not to bring his own pink slip to anybody's attention.

And then it started to make sense to Carissa. She made a note to think about it more in detention later that night.

Except she didn't get the chance. For it so happened that Isabel had accidentally sneezed in Mr. Leeland's face during her math class, and everybody knew that Mr. Leeland was a total germaphobe. So Isabel was sitting next to Carissa in the cafeteria after school for one hour while doing homework...or hardly working, in their case. The proctor had taken the fifteen or so's cell phones at the start of detention, and there was no talking, but that didn't prevent Isabel and Carissa from passing notes beneath the desk, especially when the proctor dozed off after five minutes.

So you seriously didn't see Mac at all today? Isabel wrote. Carissa shook her head. *Apparently he was on the sick list. I thought I told you that at lunch.* But as soon as she had written those words, Carissa knew that she was wrong -- Isabel had spent the entire lunch period scheming up ways to get tickets to the sold out D.V. Crew concert downtown later that month. Carissa hadn't wanted to partake in any of the insanity, but as a good friend should, she had listened to the entire plan and nodded her head when appropriate.

You didn't, Isabel said, not bringing up the D.V. Crew. *You just kind of sat there.*

Carissa tried not to roll her eyes. *I hope he's here tomorrow,* she wrote. *My detention wasn't on the office list, so the only reason I'm here is because I made them aware of it.* She paused, then scribbled *But I'm glad you're here.*

Me too! That's so weird that it wasn't on the list.

I know, right? But I should tell Mac so he doesn't have to do his detention.

That's true. Detention blows. So, are you guys really dating?

Carissa almost jumped a mile when she read what Isabel had written. *No,* she wrote. *I barely know the guy! Besides, you said he was a geeky white kid, remember?*

Well yeah. He's not my type at all. But you can't stop talking about him.

Carissa paused to try and argue Isabel on this and found she couldn't. Isabel was right about at least that -- even though she didn't believe in any of Carissa's adventures, they, and by default Mac, were all Carissa could talk about. Maybe that was why everybody thought that they liked each other. It made her remember what she had discovered in the office.

I think reality is doing some weird things, she wrote to Isabel. *It's not following the rules.*

Isabel gave her a weird look. *What do you mean, it's not following the rules?*

Think about it. The lady keeps showing up in all these places. And she was on the train this morning. Plus, not only did nobody see the thing at Saint Arbucks, nobody believes that Mac got the roof key from Mr. Withrow -- and DON'T TELL ANYBODY ABOUT THAT, she scribbled in big letters.

Ok, was all Isabel wrote.

But also, our detentions weren't written in the book. I don't know, it seems like some sort of conspiracy.

It sounds like you've been eating too many of your mama's churros.

Carissa sat still for a moment. The accident, meeting Mac on the roof, their escape, seeing the lady again at Saint Arbucks. The trip to Brooklyn, Kofenya, Dan. Peter in her hallway last night and having to call the cops.

Her eyes widened. *We have to go over to the basketball court after this.*

Isabel's eyes widened and smiled, and Carissa knew why. *To watch Eduardo practice?*

Sure, as long as we do something else first. I think I have a way to prove to you all of this is happening.

The basketball court was mostly empty when Carissa and Isabel got there, finally free from detention. To Isabel's dismay, Eduardo (*el primer bonito en el colegio*, according to Isabel) was

63

no longer there, but Peter was. He was looking over a clipboard and Carissa figured he was going over plays.

"Hey, Peter," she asked.

The tall guard player looked up from his paper. "What do you want?"

"Tell Isabel here how good my mama's churros are," Carissa said, confident that her plan would work no matter what answer she got.

Peter gave her a strange look. "Your mother's what now?"

"You know. You gave me this last night. At my apartment." Carissa pulled the pink sheet of paper out and held it for Peter to read.

He looked it over. "The roof? I thought the only person allowed on the roof was Mac Taggart, 'cause Mr. Withrow gave him a key."

Carissa looked over at her best friend, who looked to be in utter shock. She grinned. "So you weren't at my apartment at all last night?"

"Dude. I don't even know what borough you live in, much less your nabe. You're freaking me out, Lopez. And I know nothing about your mom's cinnamon rolls or --"

"They're churros."

"Whatever. The point is, it wasn't me."

"Okay. One last question -- when you woke up this morning, did your head hurt?"

Peter paused for a moment and rubbed his head in the exact same spot that Mac had hit him the previous night. "Come to think of it, it did. Kind of hurts now."

Carissa turned to a still shocked Isabel. "I rest my case."

9

The OT3 Emerges

Friday, January 11th started out as any normal day did. Carissa woke up on time, got dressed, and caught the correct train to school. Everything seemed normal, except Mac still wasn't at school when she got there. That, and she hadn't stopped by Saint Arbucks for her chai in a few days, and she was starting to miss it.

She arrived in science class and had her first surprise of the day -- pop quiz. Carissa hated pop quizzes. Mrs. Anders was notorious for them, and she should have been a little bit more prepared. She slinked back in her seat and sighed. She was usually pretty good in life science, but with everything that had been going on with her adventures, she had been more than a little preoccupied.

Mrs. Anders passed out the quiz, and Carissa took a deep breath. The quiz was on a lab they had done last week, also reviewing some advanced functions with the scientific method, and she knew that she could answer at least half of the questions. The problem was that she couldn't answer the other half.

She grabbed for her duffel, going to get a pencil out, and she noticed the other surprise of the morning. Sitting in the tray under her desk was a small piece of paper, folded up, with her name on it. Was it from Isabel? Carissa reached for the piece of paper, but stopped when she heard Mrs. Anders call out another student's name.

"Gary," she said, "you know there is no assistance on pop quizzes."

"I know," Gary said. "My pencil broke."

"Then let me get you a new one," Mrs. Anders said as Carissa quickly grabbed the pencil case out of the front of her bag. The note would have to wait. And wait it did, as that note was all Carissa could think about for the rest of the quiz.

She ended up making up answers for the rest of the questions -- one she was certain she could get some points on, but the other she knew she had no clue. She sighed as class ended and was finally able to pull out the note, stuffing it in her duffel before leaving. She had waited that long, she could wait until she got to Mr. Withrow's class and see what it said.

But she was distracted in Mr. Withrow's class as well -- because Mac was back. He was sitting in the back of the room in his normal seat, looking in a textbook, when Carissa stepped in. The problem was that he didn't even look up when she entered, and she felt a sudden shock. What if Mac was now part of this "reality doing weird things" phenomenon? What if he didn't even remember their adventures, who she was? She had to get his attention somehow -- reminding herself that, in this world now, Peter had never been in her house and they had been allowed to be on the roof. She reminded herself to tell Mac when she got a chance that he didn't have to take the now fake detention if he didn't want to.

That is, if he still remembered who she was.

"What's that?" Isabel asked when they finally sat down to lunch. She peered over at the note that Carissa now had in her hands.

Carissa ate a bite of her chicken sandwich before shooing Isabel out of her face. "Be nice. I thought this was from you. Apparently not." She swallowed. "Haven't had a chance to read it at all this morning with that pop quiz."

"I know." Isabel sighed. "I definitely failed mine."

"You would do better on those pop quizzes if you actually paid attention in class instead of reading People En Español all day."

"I know, I know." Isabel rolled her eyes and ate some of her own chicken sandwich. "So what does this note say?"

Carissa unfolded the note and dropped her chicken sandwich. The note was a plain sheet of paper, divided into two halves down the middle. On the left side was a picture, vividly detailed and hand drawn, of a girl and a boy on a bike -- and Carissa recognized it as Mac and herself. On the other side of the paper was written, in neat handwriting, "Stay away from Saint Arbucks or else."

Carissa felt her blood run cold, especially when she saw the small apple drawn at the lower right hand corner of the page. How had the lady gotten this to her? Probably the same way she had changed the train on her yesterday: magic, or something like it.

"That has got to be the most detailed and yet the most creepy drawing I have ever seen in my entire life." And before she knew what was happening, someone from behind Carissa took the sheet of paper from her and looked at it. Carissa whipped around and was surprised and glad to find Mac there.

"Dios mio," she muttered. "If it had been anybody else..."

"Where did you find this?" Mac asked as he sat it down on the table and sat across from Carissa and Isabel, where there was plenty of space for him.

Carissa blushed. "Under my seat, in science class."

"Under your seat?" Mac put the piece of paper down and pulled out a sandwich from seemingly nowhere. "Why was it there, of all places?"

"Don't know. But it's clearly for me, and you, as you can see by the message." Carissa was surprised that she was so excited to have Mac here. Now, at least, she could try to sort out this entire mess with someone who knew and believed the entire story --

"Do you believe this crazy stuff my spirit sister is making up, or are you just saying you do to get in good with her?" That came straight from Isabel's mouth as she grinned.

Carissa rolled her eyes. "Isabel, don't do this."

"¿Hace qué?"

"And don't speak in Spanish when you know Mac probably can't understand you. Heck, I can't understand you when you go on sometimes." Carissa turned to Mac. "Do I have that right? I didn't want to assume."

"It's okay. I took French, so you assumed right. I know more Russian than Spanish, from living near Brighton Beach, but I'm not conversational in either. Do you both live in the same neighborhood?"

Isabel nodded. "I'm Dominican. This Boricua and I have been spirit sisters long before we were even born. By all accounts we should hate each other, but we don't. Our grandmothers met in the market in the Heights years and years ago, shortly after my grandparents got off the boat."

Mac looked at Carissa. "Your grandparents came here from Puerto Rico?"

Carissa nodded. "It was some time before a lot of people started coming from that area, from what they used to tell me. They died a few years ago, and I still live in their apartment from all the way back then."

Mac seemed in shock; he pulled himself together the best he could and unwrapped his sandwich, which was clearly from the deli on the corner. "So you've been telling your friend all about our adventures?" he asked, completely changing the subject. "Your...what did you call her..."

"Spirit sister. Isabel, this is Mac Taggart, better known as that kid you noticed in class one day. Mac, this is Isabel Louisa Maria Gonzalez."

Isabel grinned. "I remember. The geek."

Carissa ate a bite of her chicken sandwich before she said anything that she would later regret. Mac nodded. "I'll admit, I'm a bit of a geek. But that doesn't mean I'm stereotypical."

"Prove it," Isabel said as she stole a fry from Carissa's tray.

Mac smiled and stole a fry as well. "I'm sitting here, aren't I?"

Carissa gave Mac and Isabel a cross look. "Seriously, guys. Those are mine."

"Whatever." Isabel stole one more fry. "So, you two are serious about this changing reality thing or what not?"

"Precisely," Mac said. "We were the only ones who were witness to something. Several things, at this point."

"And you remember when we talked to Peter," Carissa noted to Isabel. "Which, by the way, Peter remembers nothing about the roof or my house. Your detention notice is also invalid, by the way. So don't go. There's no record of it in the book."

"Oh. That's weird."

"Yeah. When I asked them about it, they couldn't find it, but since I still had a slip they made me go. It wasn't so bad, though, because Isabel was there too."

Isabel smiled. "So wait, this means that things you thought were real actually aren't."

Mac gave Carissa a strange look. "It's actually the opposite, where we know it's real but everyone else --"

"So that means it's possible that there are things in my own life that aren't real, either. Like me sneezing in the teacher's face the other day. Or when I tried to tumble dry my high heels at the laundromat. Or when I accidentally measured wrong in chemistry class --"

"All of those things were real," Carissa said. "This all started when I went to Saint Arbucks on Monday morning and that guy -- the one who died -- gave me my duffel back. Before then, reality is fine. After, though...I'll admit it's kind of gotten to be a mess."

"A very interesting mess," Mac noted.

Carissa sighed. "I wish I had a chai."

"Oh! Want to go to Saint Arbucks to get one after school?" Isabel asked.

Carissa peered at Isabel. "After what that note said? And how the creepy lady is always there? I'll pass."

"Maybe," Mac said, a smile now on his face. "But I do know of at least one other place you can get chai, even if it's out of the way."

Carissa smiled as she remembered. "That's true. Hey, Isabel, you mind taking the 2 train down to Borough Hall after school today?"

10

Back To Kofenya

Mac had a good idea coming, and a better one when he decided to take the subway back into Brooklyn instead of taking both Carissa and Isabel on the bike. They went straight to the subway after school and took the train all the way down to Borough Hall.

"This won't be so bad to get back uptown tonight," Isabel noted as they went topside. "But why did we have to come all the way to Brooklyn again?"

Carissa grinned. "You'll understand when you get there."

Kofenya was hopping today; there were several students there studying and almost all of the chairs and tables were taken. Carissa quickly took a seat at a small table with two chairs and put her duffel bag on the second chair to reserve their space. She knew that not everybody in their group would be able to sit down just yet, but at least she was trying.

Sure enough, Mac didn't mind standing. "Isabel ordered for you," he said. "Didn't miss a beat."

"I told you," Isabel said as she sat down and flipped her straight dark hair, "we're spirit sisters! I know everything about Carissa."

Mac laughed. "You weren't kidding."

"Well, duh. I don't kid. I get distracted. There's a

difference." Isabel relaxed in the chair. "Where's that piece of paper you guys were eyeing, anyway?"

Carissa reached back into her bag, now on the floor, and pulled it out. Mac took another look at it. "Did someone draw this?" he asked. "It looks like they did, but if it's pencil, I don't want to smudge it."

"I don't know if it's smudgable," Carissa said as a barista -- the same curly haired guy who had been studying the Bible the last time -- brought them their drinks. Carissa immediately had her hands on her chai, taking a long sip. Yep, just as good as the last time, with that special kick to it that she couldn't identify. "But it's definitely a sign, and I think we should pay attention to it."

"Does this mean you guys have to stay away from all the Saint Arbucks, or just the creepy one?" Isabel asked.

"That's a good question," Mac said as he took a long swig from his Italian soda. "For now, we should be careful and just stay away from all of them."

"Aww," Isabel said just as Carissa said, "I'm not complaining."

"What we need to do is make a list of the strange things that have happened so far, and then try to analyze them," Mac said. "I'd like to see if there are any patterns with this reality thing, and then we can try to find a solution to stop it. If people keep doing stuff and not knowing it's happening or completely forgetting, then our sense of reality is going to be well disturbed.

We need to figure out what is reality, and what is not."

"I agree," Carissa said as she took out her science notebook. Turning it to a blank page, she began to write.

"Guy collapsed at Saint Arbucks, Monday morning. Peter Doyle shows up at my apartment, Wednesday night. Two detention notices were signed for us being on the roof, Wednesday afternoon."

"Mr. Withrow remembering he gave me the key," Mac noted. "He forgot for all of Wednesday."

"So part of Monday and a lot of Wednesday were disturbed," Carissa noted. "I wonder..." She made another column and started to write, "Times I've Seen the Creepy Lady." Then she began to write again. "Monday morning at the scene of the crime. Tuesday morning when Isabel and I went for our regular. Wednesday afternoon when Mac and I stopped by to try and get clues, she was standing talking to a police officer." She put her pen down. "Which you still haven't explained, by the way."

Mac glared at Carissa, and she knew she wouldn't be getting an answer now. "Keep writing."

"I dreamed about her Tuesday night, but that was just a dream. Still gonna note it though. And then..." Carissa couldn't decide whether or not to add the strange train ride to school on Thursday. It had been like something out of a science fiction movie. Had it even been real? Then again, she had put down an incident that she knew was a dream, so... "I think I saw her on the train on Thursday. But I don't know if it was real or not."

"You didn't mention this," Mac said. "I'm pretty sure this lady is somehow involved, considering she keeps showing up and she's in that picture we found. What happened on the train, Carissa?"

She tried to remember the best she could. "She was the only person on the 1 train," she said. "And it wasn't even a real 1 train, it was a new train with the announcements and blue seats and stuff. Anyway, she knew my name, and she said that I had to figure out a puzzle and that I had to be the only one to do it. Something like that. I don't remember a lot of the details. I thought it was a dream, because --" She almost jumped as she remembered. "Because all of a sudden on the train, when she was done talking to me, the train went back to normal. It was old again and it was packed like sardines."

"Woah," Mac said at the same time Isabel said, "Eww."

"So there's that," Carissa said. "And we're, I'd say, 95% sure that this drawing is connected to her. Something's going on that is making people forget stuff, and this lady has something to do with it. And she wants me to find out what it is. By myself." She groaned. "I never was good at problem solving."

"We'll both help you," Mac said.

Isabel gave Mac a strange look. "We? Um, excuse me, but somebody's gotta go home and watch her telenovelas and play Farmtown online and..." She saw Carissa's face. "Do homework, yeah. I'm way too busy with homework to help you guys find your creepy lady."

Carissa rolled her eyes. *"Dios mio."*

"Well, I think it's fine for us to help," Mac said, "even if it's supposed to just be Carissa who finds out the secret of the world. What do you say?"

"Sounds good to --"

Carissa never got a chance to finish her sentence. Without warning, her chai tipped over and spilled all over her white duffel. She immediately stood up in shock and picked up her bag to try and save it, but it was way too late. She bit her lip. "And I've been doing so good with it, too." She sighed.

"Take it into the bathroom," Mac said. "You should at least be able to soak the top layer."

"Soak my bag?" Carissa felt despondent. "I've been trying to keep this bag clean for months now! You know how easy it is for something white to turn not white? It's a lost cause."

Isabel got up from her seat and grabbed the bag. "I'll clean it," she said. "You just sit here with *'su novio'* and I'll take care of everything." With that, she disappeared into the bathroom.

"He's not my boyfriend," Carissa muttered -- loud enough for Mac to hear.

"Is that what she said?" he asked.

She nodded. "She's always boy crazy, though. Don't let it bother you."

"Oh, I won't." Mac took the paper and put it carefully into his pocket. "We'll talk about safe topics, like math."

"Don't bore me, Mac."

"I'm not trying to. Quite the opposite, in fact."

Isabel returned shortly with the bag, which was a bit damp and still showed signs of staining. Carissa still wasn't happy; Mac decided it was best they call it a day before more coffee was spilled. Before they left, though, Isabel remembered one crucial thing that, up to this point, Carissa had forgotten.

"You don't have his phone number?" she asked, and without warning, she stole Mac's phone and started pressing buttons. "There -- now he will have both of our numbers."

With that, Isabel and Carissa returned to Manhattan, where Carissa stopped at a Bleecker Liz store and picked up some bleach for her mother. She would have to take a different bag to school tomorrow, probably the backpack she had used up until she had gotten the duffel.

When she got off the train she noticed that she had a text message from an unknown number. Unlocking her phone, she saw that it was Mac.

"Just checking to make sure that this is the correct number," the text read.

Carissa smiled. "Yep," she texted back. "Isabel can be a little bit crazy sometimes, but she wouldn't play tricks on me. Or you."

The night was uneventful; Carissa tried her best to wash her bag in the washer that her building provided for the tenants. She didn't use straight bleach, afraid that it would do more harm than good. It worked -- kind of. Most of the stains were not visible to the naked eye, save for one that ran along the side pocket that had set pretty well by the time Carissa had gotten home.

"You pick and choose your battles," Carissa thought out loud to herself.

She fell asleep and dreamed not of the creepy lady, but of the weekend to come. Weekends were usually spent with Isabel, shopping either in their neighborhood or going down to Harlem. Anywhere south of 59th Street was, in Isabel's words, "too touristy, and we go to school down there, so it's weird." Carissa had to agree, at least about the school part.

She woke up, threw on a pink skirt and a black colored blouse, then went into the kitchen where her empty duffel was still sitting from the previous night. She grabbed her coat from the rack -- then stopped.

Looking closer at her duffel, she noticed that any trace of the chai incident was gone, including all of the stains. She opened the bag, but there were no notes, no tampering. It was just gone as if she had never spilled the chai in the first place.

"Wait until I show Isabel," she said to herself as she grabbed the duffel.

11

Penguin Socks

Isabel's face was in complete shock when Carissa showed up on 125th Street within the next hour with her stark white duffel on her shoulder.

"But...but...but but but but --"

"Speechless?" Carissa grinned. "I told you this was happening. And now you have even more proof."

Isabel looked over the bag. "It's not a new one, is it?"

"*Dios mio*, no. This bag was limited edition, remember? The only place I can get a new one is online, and that would take days to get here."

Isabel nodded. "Okay, okay," she finally said, though Carissa knew that she was still shaken inside. Sure, Peter Doyle could play around, maybe even lie, but this was physical proof that this reality altering was happening.

She shouldered her bag. "Maybe I shouldn't have brought this today..."

"Oh, you're fine. I'm just...a little surprised, that's all."

Carissa grinned. "I know what can take your mind off of it."

They spent the rest of the morning checking out stores. Isabel, as usual, ended up blowing all of her money at the first store they went to, and didn't even have enough for their usual lunch at Taco Rocko (which meant that Carissa was paying again). Carissa thought about getting a new dress, but she didn't know when she would wear it, especially in this cold weather. She did, though, get a new pair of socks with penguins on them. Since they were socks, she could wear them at school. The dress code was pretty specific when it came to the actual clothing, but socks were free game as long as they didn't show above the shoe. That meant her penguins could peek out from under her shoes all day, but over the knee penguins were out.

"I gotta admit, those are cute socks," Isabel said over their Taco Rocko meals.

Carissa nodded as she ate her burrito. "I don't know when you're going to have all the time to wear those new clothes, but you'll think of something, I'm sure. You always do."

Isabel grinned. "Where are we going next?"

"Home. You're out of cash."

On Monday, the two girls went to the local coffee shop to get their drinks before going downtown for school. Since Saint Arbucks was out, if they wanted their morning buzz, they had to go elsewhere. This place had pretty good drinks and a nice atmosphere, but they were always jam packed and busy at this hour. Carissa and Isabel had to get up fifteen minutes early just in order to make their train on time.

"Take a look at this," Isabel said as she whipped out her language arts notebook. Carissa grabbed it once they were both seated on the train and turned to the page Isabel had clearly marked with a pen. There was a huge list in Isabel's handwriting, going down the entire page, with bullet points and small notes made in the margins.

"I worked on it all this weekend, when we weren't hanging out," Isabel said. "I didn't want you to see it. I wanted it to be a surprise."

"Oh, I'm surprised all right," Carissa said as she looked at the "What's Real And What's Not" title at the top of the page. "I'm so surprised that I can't even tell what the entire thing is."

"Of course you can! It's written right there at the top of the page. It's a list that I have compiled of incidents in history that people don't believe happened. I did my research. Granted, most of it was on the internet, but I tried to go only to real news sites."

"Wikipedia isn't a real news site, according to Mrs. Bellemore and the student handbook," Carissa noted as she finally saw the bottom footer littered with sources.

"I know, but this isn't class. Anyway, I'm guessing that maybe these people went through something like we're going through right now, since they don't believe these things happened. And who knows? Maybe they're right. Maybe these things actually didn't happen."

"Isabel, you have September 11th on there. That totally happened." Carissa knew this for a fact; the only thing she remembered about that day was being picked up from kindergarten by her father and walking all the way home. She didn't properly know what that day was until she asked a few years later.

"So? There are people -- most of them not in New York -- who believe it never happened."

"So what, they just believe Ground Zero doesn't exist? It does, Isabel. We've been there as a class."

"But they don't live in New York. They can't see it for themselves. And it is like you, because you say the guy collapsed and nobody else saw it."

"Except for Mac."

"Yep! Except for the white guy you can't stop talking about."

"I'm not talking about HIM, I'm talking about the fact that we both saw something nobody else did."

"Just like the people on this list!"

Carissa gave up and looked at the rest of the list. "Elvis and Michael Jackson are still alive...we never landed on the moon...the Holocaust? Seriously?"

"As well as the two World Wars, the USSR existing, and the Armenian genocide. Which I didn't even know happened until I looked it up. There's more stuff there, too."

Carissa finally just closed the book. "Tell you what, why don't we look at this during lunch? I'm sure Mac would love to see this list."

"See! You're talking about him again!"

Mac, thankfully, was more forgiving about the list than Carissa had been. He had patience stored in reserves, taking time during their lunch hour to read the entire thing all the way through, in between bites of pizza. "I heard about the Abraham Lincoln one," he said. "There are some people who believe that he turned into a vampire and fought other vampires after he 'died.' Which, of course, means he's still out there."

"With Elvis and Michael Jackson," Carissa added, trying to hide the sarcasm in her voice.

Isabel still seemed proud of herself. "You gotta admit, though, it's a good list."

"And an interesting concept," Mac said. "But all of these events have been proven true with scientific fact in this world. We haven't yet been able to replicate that with our situation."

"So should we try?" Carissa asked. "You never know when a slip like this will occur. They seem to happen at random."

Mac thought for a minute, then smiled. "How about we go back to Saint Arbucks and find our lady?"

Carissa almost dropped her piece of pizza on her duffel. "What?!?" she asked, thankful her bag wasn't soiled for the second time in a row.

"You heard me. Go back to the Saint Arbucks. See if we can find our lady. All three of us should go. Make it a full effort. And if something happens, we're all in it together."

Carissa couldn't believe her ears. The last thing she wanted to do was disobey the creepy old lady and go to Saint Arbucks, especially if it meant seeing her again. "I can't think of any good reason why --"

"We'll do it!" Isabel said before Carissa could continue. She turned and gave her best friend the most serious look she could muster.

"¿Dios mio, estás loca?"

"No," Isabel answered back with a smile. *"Yo quiero Santa Arbucks."*

That conversation was how Carissa found herself in front of her usual Saint Arbucks that afternoon, at school. Mac parked his bike at the rack out front while Isabel ran inside.

"If you guys are creeped out at the idea of going in," she had said on the walk over, "I will go in and get our drinks, and then we'll, like, go to Central Park or something. You don't have to be so afraid."

Carissa breathed a sigh of relief when Isabel had went inside. Then, she remembered the last time she had been here -- also with Mac, also with the bike, and with the police officer who had chased them off the premises.

"Hey, Mac," she said, "you remember the last time we were here? What was up with that police officer? You bolted pretty quickly, like you recognized --"

"I'm going to go around the side of the building," Mac

85

suddenly said, interrupting Carissa. "Take a look and see if there's anything in particular that we can use as a clue."

So they were mystery solvers now? *All that is missing is the talking dog,* Carissa thought to herself. "No," she said, "you are not going over there. You are going to answer my question. Furthermore, do you know anything about what's been going on? These reality slips. How Isabel's suddenly involved now. You show up and weird stuff starts happening. I want answers." She then sighed. "At least about the police officer and why you ran so fast from him."

Mac sighed and ran his hand through his hair. "If I told you, I'm not sure I'd know where to start."

So there *was* something he knew. Carissa crossed her arms. "Well?"

"I don't know about the lady. Or the person who died. I'm utterly perplexed as to why reality is acting the way it is, but then again, reality has never been my friend. And I do know why that police officer in particular went after me, though I don't know why he was talking to your strange old lady."

"So who's the fuzz??" Carissa asked, voice getting louder.

Mac sighed. "This is a sign that I trust you," he said. "Nobody knows about this except me and my mother. But that police officer was --"

"Guys!!!" That was Isabel, running from the Saint Arbucks door. She had two chais and a tea in a travel tray and she looked as if she had just seen a ghost.

"Are you okay?" Mac asked.

Isabel took a deep breath. "The old lady's in there. I recognize her even though I've never seen her before. She's showed up in my dreams once or twice. She never said a thing in the dreams, but she was much younger." She took a deep breath. "She saw me, and I know she's gonna come after us."

Isabel barely got finished speaking when the ground shook beneath their feet, causing her to drop their drinks. Carissa and Mac looked past Isabel at Saint Arbucks, and they were shocked at what they saw.

12

455 Fifth Avenue

The Saint Arbucks had frozen.

And Carissa knew that she didn't mean chilly when she thought that to herself. No -- time in the Saint Arbucks had come to a literal stop. They were moving just fine, and the world around the cafe was fine as well, but inside, it was all wrong. Carissa watched as a young professional tried to enter the cafe and froze in the doorway, unable to move. And nobody else noticed but them.

She heard a sound behind her; turning, she saw that Mac was tugging on her sleeve. "You have one of those phones that can take pictures, right? We need proof of this."

She knew what he was talking about; whipping out her phone, she pulled up the camera function and snapped a photo of the frozen in time cafe. Then, she accessed it in her phone's memory, just to check and make sure it was there.

"Got it," she finally said.

Mac nodded. "Good," he said. "Though I'm still curious as to how time just froze."

"Should we go in?" Carissa asked. "No sense in avoiding the inevitable, right?"

"I don't know," Isabel said. "Place is giving me the creeps."

"Well, when you went inside and time froze, you were able to exit just fine, right?" Mac asked.

"Yeah..."

"Then you should be able to go back in there without freezing just as that one lady did. We need to figure out why --"

"What do you think you're doing here?"

Carissa looked in front of her and saw the old lady standing in the doorway. She walked out of the Saint Arbucks and toward them, also not affected by the freeze. "I thought I told you to stay away!"

Carissa pointed at Isabel. "She did it," she said. "Wasn't me."

Isabel tried to give her best innocent face. "I was just curious."

"As am I." Mac gave the lady a distinctive glare. "I'd like to know what's going on here. What's the story with this reality distortion? You seem to know what's going on, and you're involving all of us with it --"

"Silence!" The old lady stopped right in front of Mac. Despite the fact that she was a good foot shorter than him, she carried an air of authority that spoke volumes. "I am not interested in those who have been caught in the crossfire," she hissed. "I am only interested in the one who will solve the mystery."

Carissa remembered. "You mean me?" she asked.

The lady turned and looked Carissa in the eyes. She tried

not to panic until she felt someone's hand on her shoulder. Looking, she saw Isabel by her side, also looking spooked but holding on to her friend's shoulder tight. Carissa knew that Isabel was right: that as long as she and her spirit sister were together, everything was going to be fine.

"This thing I've got to figure out...it's the same thing that you talked about on the train that one morning, am I right?"

"You are right," the lady said. "But you forget so easily. You must take this seriously, Carissa Lopez. It must be you and only you who discerns. At the same time, I do realize that there are others in your midst who can see the altered reality that we do. The more people who come into contact with you, the more people that will be able to see it."

"So we're only able to see that the Saint Arbucks is frozen because of Carissa?" Mac asked.

The lady nodded. "The herald will come soon, Carissa. You must follow the clues, and you must right these realities before the fated day, or else." She reached into her grimy pocket and handed Carissa a sheet of paper. "The three of you must not come back here again together, or more people will die."

"What?" Carissa asked, but reality had returned again. The world around them was moving, and the woman in front of Saint Arbucks was walking in like nothing had ever happened.

Isabel sighed rather loudly, looking at the ground and all of the spilled drinks. "Well. So much for coffee."

"Although we now know that, I think, it's specifically this Saint Arbucks we need to stay away from," Mac said. He looked over Carissa's shoulder. "What did she give you?"

Carissa unfolded the piece of paper. Written on it was an address. "455 5th. That's it? That's all we get?"

"I guess so." Mac sighed. "You want to go there now? Do we have enough time?"

"I do," Isabel said. "I hope this place has some coffee, though. I'm mad that I didn't get any here."

"None of us should be coming back to this Saint Arbucks for a while," Mac said. "We can all take the train down."

It turned out that the place at the address didn't serve any coffee. In fact, according to Carissa's phone GPS, it was a place they knew well as they got off the train at Bryant Park.

"The library?" Carissa asked. "The crazy old lady has me going to the library?"

"Not just any library, either," Mac said as they looked up at the huge, old building with its white columns and carved lions out front. "THE library."

"Okay, so why does she have me coming here? Does she think that I'm just going to go inside and find the answer to all of our problems right here? I doubt that it's that easy. She said something about a herald -- what's that?"

"Well, clearly the person named Harold we need to speak with is in this building," Isabel said, only to be rewarded with a facepalm and a *"Dios mio"* from Carissa.

"Maybe the herald works for the library system," Mac said, oblivious to Isabel's obliviousness. "The point is, this is the address that the lady gave to you. Therefore, this is where we start."

Mac led Isabel and Carissa into the library, through the huge doors and into the lobby. After getting their bags checked, they made their way in and upstairs, into the huge reading room to regroup. They sat at a wood table under a huge chandelier. The room was fairly packed, so they were lucky to find seats.

"Why do you think she wanted me to come all the way here?" Carissa asked. "Maybe there's a book that I have to find that will help me out with this puzzle."

"Don't forget Harold," Isabel said, too loud for a normal library voice.

Carissa rolled her eyes. "For the last time," she said. "Please."

"When we're done here, can we stop by the nearest Saint Arbucks? I still want a coffee."

"I promise we'll get a coffee! We just need somewhere to start here!"

"Excuse me?" There was a man now standing by the wood table with an inquisitive look on his face. He had a badge on with the name "Raz" on it, which made Carissa believe this young man might work at the library. "Is there anything I can help you find here?" he asked.

She decided to go for it. "Look," she said, "are there any rare books here? You know, super rare, like there's no other book like it in the entire world. I have to do this, um, school project on something unique, and I thought I'd start here. But I really don't know what's in your collection. Is there anything that you would recommend?"

The man named Raz thought for a minute, then seemed to get an idea. "You could always do your project on our copy of the Gutenberg Bible," he said. "It was one of the first printed Bibles ever. That makes it one of the oldest books in existence."

"Wow," Isabel said. "That's actually really cool. Hey, do you know any people named Harold?"

Without any warning, the fire alarm went off. Raz looked up at the high ceiling. "I have to go," he said as he ran off.

"Well," Carissa said, "nothing surprises me anymore." She got up from the table just as the intercom came on.

"Ladies and gentlemen, this is not a drill," the voice said. "There is no fire, I repeat, there is no fire in the building, but this is an evacuation. Please make your way to the nearest exit as soon as possible."

Carissa, Mac, and Isabel went along with the intercom's announcement and exited the building. "Five dollars and a chai that nobody remembers this happened," Carissa said as they joined the crowd on Fifth Avenue.

"Agreed," Mac said as he spotted the worker Raz nearby. He went up to him. "Did everybody get out?" he asked.

"They're still working on it," Raz said. "Apparently the situation is really bad. Something about one of the books was stolen. I didn't get a chance to know or hear which one."

Carissa's eyes widened, a spark in them. "Mac, where's your bike?" she asked.

Mac pointed to their left. "On the bike rack over there. Why?"

"I'll bet you two chais that the Gutenberg Bible was the book that was stolen, and if we move quickly, maybe we can catch him."

Mac's eyes widened. "Are you sure?"

"Don't ask how I know this! This is an altered reality we're dealing with. If I was going to steal a book from the library, how would I escape?"

"In a white truck," Mac said as a white truck passed them on 41st Street. Carissa watched the truck go by.

"How ironic would that be," she said, but then gasped as she saw the logo on the side of the truck. "Mac! It's that one! We need to go NOW."

Mac's eyebrows raised. "I don't quite get your logic, but I'll go get the bike."

"Good idea. Isabel, the bike's only gonna fit Mac and me. How about you go find the nearest Saint Arbucks branch and get us a seat? We're in Midtown. There has to be one on every street corner."

Isabel seemed surprised. "Where? What are we doing? Why do we have to leave?"

Carissa pointed at the truck's logo: a huge green apple. "That's why."

13

Wild Goose Chase

Mac didn't waste any time. He was back around and at the front of the library within seconds. "Take this with you," Carissa told Isabel as she gave her her duffel. "I have my phone. Tell us where you end up going."

Isabel took the duffel from Carissa. "Are you sure about all of this? I don't know if I'm being much of a help..."

"Isabel, the best way you can help us right now is by taking my duffel so it doesn't get in the way, and finding us a place to meet up in a bit. Got it?"

Isabel nodded. "I'll try," she said as Carissa hopped on the back of Mac's bike. Mac powered the bike on, and they were off. The bike started to fly down the street, cutting across the flow of traffic and down Fifth Avenue.

"Hold on tight," Mac yelled over the jet stream. "I'm gonna push this as fast as we can go. You're positive it's that truck with the green apple on it?"

"Yeah," Carissa yelled back. "It makes sense, right? Like it's a sign."

"Okay. I can see the truck roof, but it's a few streets down. We'll have to pick up the pace. You got a better grip?"

Carissa wrapped her arms around Mac's neck, thankful that she didn't have her duffel with her. "Go."

The bike shot forward as Mac upped the speed considerably, eyes forward and focused. Carissa held on for her life as they zoomed through Herald Square, past the Flatiron Building and towards Union Square. Mac was a force to be reckoned with today on the bike, and Carissa thought he was being reckless until he dove with perfect accuracy between two cars at an intersection. It was then that she realized he was just good at what he was doing.

They powered forward and, at Union Square, Mac was able to finally catch up with the truck. "There it is," he said as they pulled up right behind it. "Now what do we do?"

Carissa tried to think. "We need to follow it now closely until it stops," she said. "That way, we can find a way in."

"Sounds good. We don't want to tip them off that we're on their tail." He slowed down and followed the truck at a close distance, but not too close that it was apparent they were stalking it, from Union Square past Houston and into the Financial District. Carissa held on tight the entire time, scared that if she even thought about letting go for a moment, she would fall.

"There!" Mac yelled as she saw the truck take a sudden right turn. She held on tighter as Mac went around the corner --

and right in front of Peter Doyle.

Mac slammed on the brakes, and Carissa was almost thrown from the bike. She looked over Mac's shoulder and gasped. "What are YOU doing here?" she asked, visibly annoyed.

"Aren't you supposed to be in practice or something?"

Peter was in a heavy coat and his school slacks; he shrugged. "I am," he said, "but I got this piece of paper today in class that said to come here after school. I figured that maybe they would be shooting a reality series here or something so I thought I'd check it out."

"And where did you find this?" Mac asked as Carissa took the piece of paper by force.

"It was on the floor, like someone would have dropped it --"

"Aaaaaargh! *Dios mio!!*" Carissa threw the piece of paper on the floor. "There's a freaking apple on that page! That lady is running us around in circles!! I swear the next time I see her I will --"

Carissa had forgotten that all three of them were standing in the middle of the street.

The yellow cab didn't have that luxury. It never saw them as it barreled right toward them.

She opened her eyes to the smell of chai.

Carissa almost fell out of her chair, but realized that, much to her surprise, she was sitting in a chair. She fought to get her regular breathing pattern back. "What?"

Looking around the place she was now in, she realized that she was in a Saint Arbucks, but not her normal one. This one was much narrower and had more empty chairs than the one she was used to. Isabel was sitting across from her, sipping on what looked like a latte.

She took a deep breath. What had just happened? Had Mac and she been hit by the yellow cab? Was she dead? Was this heaven? Or had that all been a dream? Had reality reset again?

"Isabel?"

The other girl almost dropped her latte at the mention of her name. Looking over at Carissa, she gave a happy sigh. "Phew! *Dios mio, chica.* You had me scared there for a moment. When did you get back?"

It wasn't a dream. Carissa took another deep breath. "We shouldn't be back. This is weird." She quickly told Isabel about what had happened up until when she had mysteriously arrived back at this Saint Arbucks without any pause in time. "How long have you been waiting here?"

"Waiting? I just got here." Isabel took another sip of the latte. "Girl, this just keeps getting weirder and weirder."

Carissa paused for a moment as she realized an important component was missing. "Wait -- where is Mac?" And without a doubt, she feared the worst: the reality slip had only applied to her, and much like the first guy she had seen collapse in the first Saint Arbucks, Mac was no longer in this world --

Then, with no explanation what so ever, he was seated at their table, eyes closed, like he had just been taking a nap and nothing had gone wrong at all. She touched his shoulder. "Mac?"

He opened his green eyes, and they met her brown ones. And without any warning, he grabbed Carissa and pulled her out of her chair and into his arms.

The world was silent around them. If Carissa stopped breathing for a pause, she could hear Mac's heartbeat, proof that he, too, was alive. "You're okay," he whispered, and she suddenly understood how close she had been to death.

Maybe they hadn't been supposed to chase that truck. Maybe they had tried to find another way. The apple on the truck may have been a false alarm. Either way, the reality slip had taken care of them. But Carissa didn't expect it to always be this easy. Next time -- and with how that lady spoke, there would be a next time -- they would have to be more careful.

"You're okay, too," she whispered, startled as to how soft her voice sounded.

"Ummmmm...did I miss anything while you guys were on the bike?" That was Isabel. "Because you guys are hanging all over each other."

Carissa separated herself from Mac and noted the blush on his face. "I'm just glad we're okay, considering the circumstances," she said.

Isabel rolled her eyes. "Whatever. I owe you guys coffee or something, right?"

Carissa texted Mac when she finally got off the train that

night, and they texted back and forth for an hour over schoolwork. Carissa had a question on her math homework, and Mac helped her with it. Carissa noted how well they worked as a team, without even trying.

Before she went to bed, she stayed up with her family to watch the eleven o'clock news...which meant that they were watching on Telemundo. Oh, well. And sure enough, there was something on the news about a robbery at the New York Public Library. The Gutenberg Bible was still out there, somewhere. They hadn't found it. But at least they now knew it was important, and the burglary had survived the reality slip.

She texted Mac about it before she fell asleep. "It bothers me," she wrote. "I'm tired of this. I want answers."

"Let me think about it tonight," Mac said. "I'll let you know if I figure out anything in the morning. How about all three of us sit together at lunch?"

Carissa smiled. "Sounds like a plan."

She then changed out of her day clothes, brushed her teeth and went to bed. It wasn't every day that somebody saw time freeze in a cafe, then got involved in a bike chase and almost got hit by a taxi. Carissa needed some serious sleep.

But she didn't get it. That night, Carissa had a dream about the truck. This time, though, instead of going downtown, it went to the zoo in Central Park. When they got there, the truck stopped and lasers shot out of the front windshield, opening all of the cages. The entire zoo went into chaos. A mother accidentally left her stroller, and Carissa had to jump off of Mac's bike and grab the baby to protect it from a horde of snakes. She looked over and saw Mac battling an orangutan with a mop handle. The old lady was there as well, just sitting there with a red apple and watching the entire thing as it was happening. This time, she didn't help out.

After she woke up, she couldn't tell which incident was what really happened, and which incident was a clear play at reality. Which was which? What she had said earlier to Mac was true. This needed sorted out, sooner rather than later. It was starting to make her head spin.

She got up early and looked outside her window. Even at this hour, there were people outside on the street...the reason she wasn't allowed out after a certain hour. Washington Heights wasn't the most spectacular place to live, but it was home. She wondered for a minute what would happen if she didn't find out what was causing all of these issues, if reality continued to do this to her. She had to figure out the puzzle before the fated day...whenever that was. Would she lose her home? Her parents? Worse?

She didn't want to find out.

14

In Case Of Emergency, Eat The Apple

The next day, thankfully, everything started out normally. Carissa went to class, failed another pop quiz, and ate lunch with Mac and Isabel.

"I still can't believe I bombed it," Carissa said. "I should have been more focused last night on the science portion of my homework instead of the math. It's my own darn fault."

"It's your own darn fault because you were on the phone last night when you should have been sleeping," Isabel noted.

"Yeah, but I was still doing something school related. Quit your complaining. Besides, I've had a headache all day. Probably wouldn't have done well on the pop quiz even if I had studied."

"You need meds?"

"I need a day off is what I need. But no, I'm okay. The headache isn't that bad. Nothing greasy food can't fix."

"You girls, we need to get down to business." Mac sighed and pulled out his notebook. He flipped to the page that said, "Time Slips." On it was a list of all of the time slips the three of them had experienced so far. "I'm still curious how we were saved from death yesterday," he said. "Nothing like that has happened in any of the other time slips."

"It was almost like we were given a second chance on purpose," Carissa said. "Like we aren't supposed to die yet."

"Correction -- you aren't supposed to die yet. You're still supposed to figure out whatever this puzzle is. And to be honest, we haven't been making much headway. We know to stay away from the Saint Arbucks on 72nd Street, and we know that things with apples on them may be a clue, from what that creepy lady was showing us. Plus, it's possible this still missing Gutenberg Bible has something to do with it. Other than that, we're on an uncertain deadline. We don't even know when this fated day is."

"Not like it's listed as a holiday," Carissa said. "That lady needs to give me more clues."

"We have plenty of clues, remember?" Isabel said. "Like the list I made. Totally valid."

Carissa glared at her spirit sister. "Are you serious?"

"What are you talking about?" Isabel asked, chewing on a fry. "It's a totally valid list. I mean, seriously, we still don't know about Tupac."

"You put Selena on that list as well," Carissa said with another eye roll. "Seriously, you need to give that thing a rest."

"Dios mio," Mac muttered.

Carissa and Isabel looked at him, then both laughed. Apparently he had been around them long enough that he was starting to pick up their language. It was enough that their other friends had taken notice, what with the way they were hogging the table all to themselves and talking secretly. While Carissa and Isabel's friend groups weren't extensive, Carissa was secretly hoping for a long term time slip for them after this entire business was done, so her friends other than Mac and Isabel would forget any of this was happening. Thankfully, with some of the slips went some of the days they went ignored, replaced in their memories with fun times, regular table packed lunches without Mac, and even one time an after school shopping trip where Isabel blew all of her (nonexistent) money again. These were events that had never happened, but were in these people's minds to take place of where the time slips were.

Carissa shook her head again. "We do need more information. The next time I get a chance, I'm gonna find that old lady and ask her exactly what she means by these clues. If I don't see her in a couple of days, I'll even risk Saint Arbucks again if it means I'll get some --"

She never got to finish her sentence -- it was drowned out by the fire alarm. Mac stood up from his seat. "Seriously?" he asked.

"Five bucks everybody forgets this," Isabel said as she got up from her seat. "Man, and I was having a good lunch, too. Maybe I'll leave it here and finish it after this drill."

Carissa paused. "Wait -- did anybody here know anything about a drill today? They usually announce those in homeroom, don't they?"

"Thought so, but they didn't say anything," Isabel said. "Why?"

Carissa grabbed her bag. "Maybe this isn't a drill."

They walked out of the cafeteria, all three of them. When they went out into the hallway, Carissa noticed that the hallway did have a strange smell to it, like one of the chemistry students had messed up an experiment again or something. She hoped that was all it was and went to file out of the school with her friends, just like every emergency drill her classes had done before.

Their hallway was supposed to lead them straight to the lobby, which would dump them on Broadway without any problems. Except nobody anticipated the hallway being blocked.

Carissa looked around herself at other students much like her, trapped on the first floor up against what honestly looked like a huge wall of flames. She wasn't sure where it had come from, except that it was blocking the hallway -- and she really hoped this moment was lost to a time slip, sooner rather than later. She took a deep breath. "Anyone up for the roof?"

"Good idea," Mac said, whipping out the key that he still had. He raised his voice. "Everyone, I know how to get out of this building from the roof. You know how they always said in the drills to go to the roof if the regular entrances were blocked? From here, the front door is our only exit, and it's not accessible. There's no exit in the cafeteria, which means we have to move up. If no helicopters come, then I can get us down. I promise. Now, who's with me?"

The crowd was silent until Isabel spoke up. *"¿Qué hacen?*

¡Vámonos!"

That got people moving. Everybody formed a line behind Mac, with Isabel going in the middle and Carissa taking up the rear, duffel still on shoulders. She saw Peter in the line, which answered another one of her questions; turned out he had also made it out fine after yesterday's close call with the taxi. She made sure the line moved smoothly as it went all the way up, from the first floor to the fourth and onto the roof itself. "Everybody okay up there?" she asked.

She didn't remember the next bit. Something like a stabbing pain in her head caused her to sit down on the stairs leading up to the roof. Carissa held her head in her hands. Not now, not now...what was causing this?

"Carissa?" That was Mac's voice. She heard footsteps coming straight toward her, and then she felt Mac's hands on her shoulders. "What's wrong?"

She shook her head. "I don't know. Something's wrong."

"Is it your headache? I remember that you mentioned you had one."

"I don't think so --" Carissa winced again as her head pounded. She leaned her head on Mac's shoulder. "It just hurts. A lot. I don't think I can walk."

"Let's get you upstairs," Mac said as he knelt by her side. "You'll have to drop the duffel, though. Can you deal?"

"Eh, I already lost it once to a chai." Carissa dropped her

duffel and held onto Mac's shoulders. Every time she moved, there was another flash of pain through her brain. "I don't know how this could have suddenly come on. I was fine a few minutes ago."

"The only thing I can think of that would be causing this may be..." Mac shook his head. "No, that can't be right."

"What is it?"

"Maybe yesterday's close call wasn't so close. Maybe we still got hit, but we don't remember it. And just now, you're starting to feel the effects of it. If that's so, then we need to get you on the roof as soon as possible."

"Why?" Carissa had to shut her eyes, the pain making it too hard to see now.

"Because if you have a concussion, then you have to go to the emergency room right now. I'm not losing my partner to a crash that never happened."

It didn't really, but for Carissa, it felt like time actually stopped as Mac said those words. "I'm your partner?"

A pause. "Well...yeah. You're the only thing making sense to me in this world where everything can change in the drop of a pin. No offense, but a lot has been changing these days. I need you as my constant, Carissa." And Mac picked her up, but he held her too close for the act to be simple.

Carissa tried to think straight. "What do you mean?"

She was interrupted by the sounds of something crashing.

She tried to open her eyes but found she couldn't. "What was that?"

"You...don't want to know," Mac said, and the tone of his voice was not good. "We have to find another way out. The stairwell's been blocked."

She tried not to panic. This was their current reality, but there had to be another way. "Are there any other exits?" Mac's silence told her exactly what she needed to know. So now all they had to do was cause a time slip. But how? If Carissa was in charge of figuring these things out, then she should do a better job of keeping track.

She gasped. "Mac, this is a stretch, but it might work. I need you to get me back down to the cafeteria."

"Why?"

"Just do it! My head still hurts!"

Mac didn't say another word, but Carissa felt herself being moved, and then her head was pushed right up against his chest as he ran. And man, did Mac run fast. She tried her best to focus on her breathing, but even that was hard now. There had to be too much smoke in the air.

"Okay, we're here," Mac said as he barreled through a door and sat Carissa down on a table. "Now what?"

"Find me an apple. Doesn't matter which kind, just find me one!"

Carissa fought through her headache and tried to open her

eyes. She finally got them open just as Mac put an apple in her hands. Her eyes met his as she took a bite, praying that something would happen.

With the crunch, the world around them stopped.

15
Survival Tactics

Sarah crossed her legs again and sipped her frapp. "Seriously? Where is he?" She leaned her head on her hand. "This is the last time he's late. I swear."

There was a light snow falling outside the Saint Arbucks that morning, a chilly one that Sarah hadn't prepared for. She huddled in the back of the cafe and drank her drink, her usual without any whip cream. The barista had curiously asked her why she was ordering a cold drink in the dead of winter, but Sarah had not responded. She had simply paid for the drink and moved on with her life. Reality was not kind to her anymore. The barista would probably forget her drink again, as they had a habit of doing, she had thought to herself. Indeed, fifteen minutes after she had placed her order, she had to show them her receipt to prove she had ordered the drink in the first place, and she received another free drink coupon good on a future order.

I think I only pay for about half of my drinks here, Sarah thought to herself as she pulled out her tablet. If he was going to be late today, of all days, then she might as well get started without him. She unlocked the screen and scrolled through the apps until she got to one with a red apple on it labeled "QWERTY." She tapped it, and it started, pulling up a file with the designation "Y-MH-560" at the top.

"Sorry I'm late."

She looked up from her tablet to find him standing there, out of breath, as if he had just used the subway to get there. "Quit your faking, Mick. You better have a good excuse for your absence."

"Does it involve paying for your next drink?"

"No. I got another blasted free drink coupon. Now sit down and show me what you've got. We don't have a lot of time."

Mick was quiet, but he nodded as he sat across from Sarah at their booth. He pulled out a cell phone from his jacket pocket and tapped a few buttons. Sarah merely gave Mick a once-over and whistled. "Going for the three piece suit look today, I take it."

"Of course. I figured I would fit right in with this neighborhood."

"And so what, you're just going to show up as Hispanic if we go to the Heights? Black in Bed-Stuy? Give me a break, Mick. You're disgusting."

Mick grinned. "I'm sent. There's a difference."

"Not on this plane of reality, there's not. Enough beating around the bush. What do you have?"

Mick handed the phone to Sarah. "This so far. We could always do a random selection with the population we're given. At this cafe, even."

"Mick, we have two weeks to pull this off. We need someone who's going to be clued in to the entire process.

Someone who can handle the merging of the realities. And someone who's going to figure out the clues we'll have to send them in a roundabout way. This is the biggest decision we'll ever have to make for this world, Mick. We can't get this wrong."

"Or else, or else, I get it, yada yada yada."

"Mick, there's a reason I was put in charge, and you just demonstrated it."

Mick took Sarah's frapp and took a sip from it without her permission. "Just look at the files," he said.

Sarah nodded and started to flip through Mick's files with her finger. Picture after picture showed smiling faces, photos taken incognito of people who didn't even know that they were getting their picture taken. There had to be at least three hundred photos in this folder alone. "Did you narrow them down at all?"

"Not exactly, but I did get one that you'll have to look at. Can I?"

"That's the first time you've asked permission on something in a long time, sweetheart," Sarah said as she gave Mick back his phone.

Mick just grinned and tapped the emerald ring on Sarah's left ring finger. "You can't be that mad at me."

"Try me."

"Especially considering the circumstances. Especially since if we pick the wrong person --"

Sarah got up from her chair and got into Mick's face. "Do

not try me right now. We made it through Project Metropolitan without anybody getting left behind, right?"

Mick just nodded. When Sarah spoke, she was right.

She sat back down. "So if we can take care of a huge project like that, then this is easy."

"Sarah, I was held hostage at the Metropolitan Opera for three months. Anything is easy after what you had to do to free me."

"Yeah, and if you bring it up again, I swear I'll break out into Nessun Dorma right here in this Saint Arbucks. Now show me what you wanted to show me."

It took Mick a few minutes to find it, but he did. "This."

Sarah took the phone from him and looked it over. It was a picture snapped of a boy, a teenager, really, with bright red hair sitting on a bike. She raised her eyebrows as the meaning made sense. "That's the Taggart boy. He's here? What's he doing outside of Coney Island?" She put the phone down. "I thought we told Rue to keep him in Brooklyn, or else. Certainly explains why things have gotten worse these past few months, though. As long as that Taggart boy isn't in Brooklyn, we're going to have problems. Unless, you know, we're able to finally resolve his own issues. How are Harley and Kiv doing on that, anyway?"

"Project's been stalled for some time. They've been busy with other things."

"Well, get them back on that. If we can get it resolved by

the fated day, maybe Taggart will actually still be alive at the end of this debacle." Sarah took another sip of her frapp. All of this thinking was making her head hurt. "No other pictures of note, other than that one?"

"None that jumped out at me. You'll have to take a look."

Sarah groaned. "Fine. But get that second frapp, then. The usual."

"Even though it's cold out?"

"Just go, Michael! Now!"

"Okay, okay." And Mick was gone, waiting in line to get Sarah another drink…even though she had another free drink coupon. Sarah rolled her eyes and turned back to Mick's phone. This would be so much easier if she wasn't engaged to her partner. She wondered what Jesse was up to these days; while she was a little flighty, Sarah and Jesse had conquered their share of projects over the years, only changing when Mick had come into the picture. Of course, it hadn't hurt that Mick and Jesse were related, and the three of them had been assigned to Project Metropolitan together.

Mick hadn't said anything recently about his sister, which usually meant she was still good with Milton. Dang. Not that being stuck with Mick was a chore. She just wished he listened sometimes.

She continued to scroll until she found a picture of a girl sitting at this same Saint Arbucks. She was young, maybe about the Taggart boy's age, Hispanic, lived up north. Her family had been in the city for generations, which meant that if Sarah gave this girl directions somewhere, she knew that they would be followed. Plus, if she went to this same Saint Arbucks often, they could start correspondence even today. It would be perfect...if she showed up.

Mick arrived back at the table, and Sarah grabbed the frapp from him. "Any luck?"

"What about her?" Sarah showed Mick the picture she had found. "She's from the city, and from the looks of it, at least she frequents this area."

"Goes to the school on the corner, too, telling from the uniform. Do you think she knows Taggart?"

"Her? No way. Rue's got him at school near Borough Hall, remember? She's got him in a lock for after schools at Kofenya. You tend to forget there are eight million people living in this city. There's no way she knows Taggart."

"Oh, right. I had forgotten that."

What had she just thought about Mick not listening? She sighed and sipped more of her frapp. "We need to make a decision. We don't have much time."

Mick's eyes widened. "Your six."

Sarah turned and saw the girl from the photo step into the Saint Arbucks, a white duffel on her shoulder. "Bingo. Are you good?"

"Of course I am. Are you?"

She kissed him quickly. "I am now. Stick around the bathroom. I'll make sure she leaves her bag in there, so you two can connect. I'll be outside." She touched him on the head and smiled, trying to hide her sadness. "See you in two weeks, sweetheart."

He smiled back as well, more confident than she that everything would work out and they would actually meet again. "Two weeks."

Carissa touched the smoke that hung in midair over the lunch table. "It...stopped."

"And so did your headache, I assume," Mac said. "We don't know how long this stop is going to last. We need to head out of here and get you to the hospital before your head starts hurting again."

"Oh, I don't think that will be necessary."

Mac and Carissa watched as a young woman walked into the room, with long blonde hair done up in a bun and a blue sundress -- in the middle of winter. She stood next to them. "The pause can last for as long as you want it to. I'm surprised you haven't figured that out yet."

"Who are you?" Mac asked. "And why are you here?"

"Why are we here," Carissa asked, eyes now closed, "standing in the middle of a burning building that's been frozen in time?"

"Because you're the one who has frozen it. And you will have that ability up until the fated day." The woman smiled. "I assume you have some questions about all of this?"

"Too many," Carissa said. "It makes my head hurt just thinking about it."

The woman sat down. "I can't leave this building, or time will restart," she said. "My name is Rue. Come along, Pond. Sit down, and I'll tell you everything I can."

16
The Basics Of QWERTY

Mac sat down on the cafeteria table. There was still smoke around them, but since they were frozen in time, they could breathe the air around them fine as it filtered in from who knew where. Carissa sat next to him, closer than either of them anticipated. "My head still hurts a little," Carissa said, and Mac let her sit close, even though he didn't know the full meaning of her statement.

He wished he did.

"So," he said, looking straight at the woman who had broken through their reality slip and crashed their party, "tell me who you are. Like, really. No fooling."

The woman nodded. "My full name is Aurora Radilla de la Pasquale, but everybody calls me Rue. You may, as well. I am an associate with the Quintessential Works for Everyday Reasons To Yield, Llorin Division, Dealey Faction."

"The what now?" Mac asked. He noticed that Carissa wasn't speaking up, most likely because her head still hurt. Very well. He was fine with interrogating this Rue solo, and he wasn't going to go easy on her.

"I told you. The Quintessential Works for Everyday Reasons To Yield. It's a top secret, cross-dimensional platform that makes sure rules and regulations are adhered to. I know all about your issues with reality, how it keeps starting and stopping, and how people don't remember it, and how you didn't know how to do it yourself even now."

Mac looked down at the apple that Carissa had taken a bite out of. He looked over at Carissa herself and saw that she had her eyes closed, probably dozing. And for good reasons. Today had been a long day. In fact, these had been several long days in a row now.

"What's with the apple thing?" he asked. "We're seeing apples all over the place now. I mean, it clearly means something, but I don't know exactly what it is. I've been trying to figure it out, but there's no simple answer. Do you know what kind of adventures we've been on?"

"I hadn't, but before I got here, I reviewed your file to make sure I understood the case," Rue said.

"Oh. File?"

"The one Carissa's representative set up."

"You're not making any sense. Can you speak in a language I can understand, please?"

"I am. I reviewed your file, so I know all of the so called adventures you and this girl have been on. I do believe you had a question for me?"

Mac tried his best to contain himself. "The apples."

"Oh. That is the symbol that Carissa's representative has set up for this project. If you see an apple, you know you're on the right track. And, as you can see, Carissa has figured out that using an apple stops the flow of this dimension, for as long as you like."

So we can get her to a hospital after this, Mac thought to himself. *Heck, I could take her and get her right there before reality starts up again.* "You keep talking about Carissa's representative. I'm just curious: is that the creepy old lady she keeps running into?"

"You would be correct. But she's not old and creepy in the dimension I call home. That's just the way she has decided to appear to Carissa."

Mac thought back to the picture of the two people that they had found, the one Dan had analyzed at Kofenya. "So that picture really was the lady, and the man who died, but in another dimension? Where the old lady is younger like she is in the photo?"

Rue nodded her approval. "You understand well, Macardle Irving Taggart. In fact, you understand so well that I bet, if your circumstances were different, then you would have been picked to assist us with this project instead of the girl."

He looked at Carissa, then back at Rue. "What are you talking about?"

"She's pretty well asleep, so I'll make this clear only once, Taggart. QWERTY monitors everything that happens in this universe, and several others that you can barely imagine. We monitor for inconsistencies and do our best to make sure they are fixed, that the rules of each universe and world are adhered to. Do you have any clue as to what I am speaking about, Mr. Taggart?"

He did. He did know. And it was something he had never spoken to anyone about. "What does my...inconsistency have to do with all of these reality slips?"

"Nothing as far as triggering them. But you remember how hard it was for you to get into this school? That was my doing. You're not supposed to be in this school, Mac. You were supposed to stay in Brooklyn. And hindsight tells us now that you were supposed to stay in Brooklyn so that you wouldn't get involved in this project that Carissa is working on. But that's free will for you. You think you know best, yet you never get the full story."

Mac was silent for a moment, digesting this latest bit of information. "What is this project that Carissa is supposed to do?" he asked. "She's received some clues from the lady saying to stay away from that Saint Arbucks, and to solve something before the fated day."

"That girl is the one out of your group with the power to bend this reality now," Rue said. "She has temporarily become one of us. Therefore, she needs to stay away from our operations base – that Saint Arbucks – or else time and space will warp on their own. And she will need to fix this reality before the chosen day, or all of the inconsistencies around her will automatically try to fix themselves."

He didn't like where this was going. "What do you mean?"

"If the inconsistencies are not fixed, they will be automatically eliminated by the system. I'm sure you understand why you can't inform her of any of this information. She must decide for herself what she is to do with this reality. There is potential for greatness here, but there is an end goal. To reach that end goal, it may be necessary for some of the inconsistencies to be eliminated anyway. But the decision is Carissa's alone. If you influence that decision and Carissa fails in her mission, you can be sure your inconsistency will be exposed."

"So...I can't tell her?"

"Precisely. And it's a bit late to try and fix your own problem, is it not?"

"I've beaten the system once before, and I'll beat it again if I have to."

"Oh, but you're not supposed to break the rules. My boss doesn't like it when people break the rules." Rue grinned and sat her head on her hands, propping it up. "Isn't that right?"

It hurt. He tried to ignore it, but it was impossible. "So what can I do?"

"Well, since you're here, you can help her with her mission. See if you can decode the clues that her rep has set up. The Saint Arbucks is her home base, as I mentioned, and that's why you can't go back there. Every time you get close, it will set off another slip, as you saw last time. Any other Saint Arbucks is fine."

"Okay. When is the fated day?"

"Nuh uh uh, you know I can't tell you that. All I can say is that it's much closer than you think. You've wasted too much time, although now that Carissa has figured out how to manipulate this dimension, you'll have a distinct advantage." Rue stood up. "And with that, I've given you all of the information I can at this time. You're doing good, Mac. Better than I thought you would be doing, considering it all."

Mac had a feeling Rue wasn't talking about just this project. "You mentioned you're my representative. What does that mean?"

As she stood in the window, the smoke seemed to glow with the way the sun hit the panes. Rue turned back at Mac. "What do you think it means?"

And then she was gone, without any warning. Time was still frozen, and Mac knew now that was Carissa's doing. What puzzle did she have to figure out? What kind of power had she been given? And what responsibility with it? He still didn't have it figured out, but he knew now that he had to.

Rue had made it painfully clear: his own inconsistency was on the line.

He touched Carissa on the shoulder. "Are you still asleep?" It then occurred to him that, maybe, Rue had done something to Carissa to make her sleep like this. Maybe that conversation they had just had had been meant for his ears only.

He would do with the information what he could. And until then, he just had to get Carissa to the hospital before things got worse.

He touched her on the shoulder again, then moved her aside and steadied himself. He reached under and lifted Carissa into his arms, holding her close. Perhaps the most important question was: who was this girl who had been thrust into his life without any warning? According to Rue, he only had a limited amount of time to figure it all out.

She stayed asleep as Mac carried her through the burning building, as he sat her sleeping form next to his bike and ran back to get her duffel. She stayed asleep as he steadied her and powered on the bike, not pedaling at all, holding her with one arm and steadying her weight with his knees, steering with the other arm. She didn't wake up as they passed by a frozen city, cars and traffic lights and people and dogs and pigeons not moving a single inch, yielding all of their power to a school age girl temporarily gifted with the literal ability to change the world.

He didn't know what this QWERTY organization was up to. All he knew was that he would help get the project done, or else.

And Carissa slept as they rode across town, to the hospital. She slept up until Mac had her safely seated in an emergency room armchair and her name written at the top of the list.

Then she -- and the rest of the world -- woke up.

17

Carissa's Mother Speaks To God

The sun peeked into the room as Carissa finally opened her eyes. The first thing she saw was the ceiling, and then the monitor beside her, and then the sight of her mother sitting on a bedside chair.

She stirred, and then her mother raised her head. The fact that she didn't immediately hug Carissa and start crying told Carissa that her diagnosis was good. It wasn't surprising that she woke up here -- she had actually woken up in the emergency room, unsure as to how she got there until Mac had explained that it was him. Then she had passed out again in that same emergency room, which meant that it also didn't surprise her now that she was hooked up to a machine.

The only thing that really surprised her was that nothing surprised her. The scene was about as normal as a scene could be...well, for being in a hospital, of course.

"You okay?" Carissa's mama asked with a smile.

Carissa nodded. "What happened?" She had a good idea of what had happened, but she wanted to hear this reality's take on it.

"Well, there was a fire in your school," Carissa's mama said. "And you hit your head and passed out. There was this white boy who got you out of the school. He said he knew who you were. They took care of the fire quickly, and it was contained to the first floor."

Carissa nodded, remembering that her mom must not know who Mac was even after the incident with Peter in her apartment. If reality could just stay still for once, then maybe she could think straight and everybody else could start seeing the same things again. But there had been that blonde haired girl in the cafeteria. Rue. And Mac had spoken to her. Had he said more after Carissa had passed out?

She hoped he had. Knowing Mac, he would probably tell her everything. She hoped. This was Mac she was thinking about, the same kid who had ran from that police officer for no reason. What was the deal with that, anyway? She still hadn't gotten a concrete answer.

She rubbed her eyes. "Did anything else happen?"

"No. They just brought you here. You had a minor concussion, and they're going to keep you here for a couple of days to make sure you're fine. But they treated everything." Carissa's mom was calm...too calm, in her own opinion. Normally, in a situation like this, Carissa would have to fight for her breath as her mama squeezed her and made sure she wasn't out of her sight again. But there was none of that.

"Mama," Carissa said, "are you sure that you're okay? You're taking this entire situation way too well."

Her mother smiled. "I had a dream last night where the Lord appeared to me," she said. "And the Virgin Mary was there as well, right next to Him. I cowered on the ground and said I wasn't worthy to see Him, but He spoke to me and said that as long as I followed Him, everything would be all right. When I heard about your accident today, at the school, I remembered that dream and realized that the Lord was preparing me for this very moment. So I have been praying this entire time, and the Lord has given me peace."

Carissa tried not to roll her eyes. Her mother was always like this, talking about God and how great He was. It wasn't that she didn't believe in Him, it was just that she had always been around other students who had believed differently than her. She wanted to figure out what she believed for herself, and she hadn't had a chance to do that yet. Quite honestly, she hadn't cared up until this entire reality thing had started.

She paused for a moment. "Mama, where is that white boy?"

"Oh, I made him sit out in the lobby with Isabel. She's here, too, and she's fine. Would you like for me to go get them?"

Oh, if Mac had to deal with Isabel and her list by himself, then Carissa needed to relieve him. "Yes please, Mama."

Isabel came into the room first and did exactly what Carissa thought her mother would have done -- wrapped her arms around Carissa and started bawling hysterically. Carissa had to roll her eyes. "Seriously, Isabel?"

"Don't say that! I was so worried about you!"

"Sure she was," an exasperated Mac said as he entered the room. He sat in the chair Carissa's mother had sat in before.

"I'm going to go call Solana," Carissa's mother said, referring to her boss.

Carissa nodded. "Okay. You do that."

The minute the door closed behind Carissa's mother, both Mac and Isabel crowded closer to Carissa. "So you really learned how to stop the world?" Isabel asked.

Carissa nodded. "Mac, did that blonde girl tell you anything important when we were in the cafeteria? I don't really remember that well."

"You wouldn't." Mac sighed. "She talked about the things that the old lady had said, that reality is doing some weird things and you are the only one who can fix it. And since you are the only one who can, then you have been given the temporary power to alter reality as well. She also said again that you need to fix it by a certain day, or else everything will be in jeopardy."

"I know, I know. Wish I knew when that day was, though. But let me fill you both in on something." And then she told Mac and Isabel about her mother's dream.

Isabel's face was in shock. "Your mama spoke to God?" she said.

"Well, not really speaking to God. More like God spoke to her in a dream. And she listened and it made her relax. Here's the thing -- I can't say for sure, but maybe I was supposed to hear about that dream." She paused. "I think maybe God has more to do with this thing than we originally thought."

"What do you mean?" Isabel asked, but there was a look of knowing on Mac's face.

"The Gutenberg Bible," he said with a smile. "Not that I had forgotten about it, but we've had more important things on our plate as of recent."

"I agree," Carissa said, "but that book has to be important somehow."

"Of course it's important. Otherwise, I wouldn't have sent you to find it."

All three turned toward the old lady, who had appeared in the room out of nowhere, still in her old clothes that hadn't been washed, now holding another red apple in her hands. She gave the apple to Mac. "You're doing well, but proceed with caution. Especially you. You've been given warning." It was the first time Carissa had seen Mac be addressed directly by the old lady.

Then, she turned to Carissa. "I will not give you any more second chances," she told her. "From now on, you must make your own second chances. These worlds will not be kind to either one of us. And if you don't do something, it will all change, and it will not be fixed." She produced another apple out of her pocket. "Shall we initiate the survival tactics?"

And then she was gone again, and Carissa wanted to scream. She wasn't getting any answers, but she thought she might know where she could find some. "Mac," she said, "I'm stuck here for a couple of days. Take Isabel with you, and find that Bible. Skip school, break as many traffic laws as you want, I don't care as long as the two of you are safe. Just find that book."

Mac nodded. "I may even call Peter on this."

Carissa's eyes widened. "Oh no you don't. You're not including anybody else in this Scooby gang."

"I might not have a choice. He came up to me earlier and asked how we got out. He knows we didn't get out by the roof, like everybody else thinks. So I think it may be time to fill him in."

Carissa sighed. "Jinkies. Fine."

Sarah completed the jump and headed back to Saint Arbucks, where she hoped that somebody would be waiting -- and they were.

"Thank goodness," she said as she high fived Rue and received her drink. "I was about to go crazy there for a minute."

"It's not easy being an interdimensional agent," Rue said as she sipped her own tea.

"It's not easy being green, either, but nobody told the Lex line that." Sarah sipped her frapp and downed a quarter of it in an instant. "Still no clues about Dvorak's whereabouts?"

"Nope. Any updates on your side? I know you just got back."

"Well, Taggart got her to the hospital okay. You have a lot of trust in that boy. I suppose it comes from being assigned to him."

Rue smiled. "I'm loyal."

"And you're loyal to me, too, which does both of us a world of good. Anyway, Taggart is gonna get another kid to help him find the Gutenberg. The Doyle guy -- he's Raz's kid. Once we get that Bible into their hands, we'll be able to decode for ourselves where Dvorak is at and send Carissa there. I'm still not sure about that other girl with Lopez, though. She seems like kind of an airhead. Rue, do you have any idea who is assigned to her?"

Rue had to think for a moment. "I think...oh! Last I heard Ariana was covering her...but that can't be right."

"Yeah, you're wrong. Let's not talk about Ariana." Sarah made a face. "Do me a favor and check on that when you can. No huge rush. Just try to get it done by tomorrow."

"Will do. Is there anything else you need help with?"

Sarah sipped her frapp again, then looked back at the ring on her finger. "Just make sure they actually do this and help us find Dvorak, before both of these worlds end up in the same limbo Mick's in right now. From the way things are going, we might actually be able to pull this one off."

18
Don't Forget Your Cricket Bat

"So remind me what we're doing again?" Peter asked.
"And why did I have to go get this cricket bat?"

"You didn't have to get it, remember?" Mac said. "I just
suggested that you go and find a blunt object that you could use in
case we get ourselves in trouble. I had thought you would bring
something like, I don't know, a frying pan? But a cricket bat
works as well, I suppose." He pointed to his bike. "You do realize
that we're riding on that thing, right?"

Peter took one look at the bike and his eyes widened. "You
have got to be kidding."

"Yeah, well, unfortunately I'm not. And you don't have a
choice if you're going to be a part of this. You do believe there's
something weird going on, right?"

"Shut up, Taggart. Of course I do. All these unexplained
things that aren't adding up just right. It makes me want a beer."

"I'm going to pretend I didn't hear you just say that." Mac
put the kickstand up on his bike. "Let's go, Doyle, before I change
my mind."

He straddled the seat, and Peter jumped on the back,
putting his feet on the rungs. In an instant, Mac wished Carissa
was here instead of the boy who had constantly made fun of him
in class all year. But then Peter's hands were on Mac's shoulders,

and he steadied himself on the bike.

He wasn't going to go easy on his adversary. "You better hold on," was all he said, and then he was off, leaving Peter holding on for dear life.

The Saint Arbucks on 72nd Street was closed, but you couldn't tell that to Sarah. She didn't have any other place to go, no home to return to in this dimension.

She drank one more frapp while sitting in the way back, where nobody could see her if they tried to look in through the dark windows. But it didn't matter anyway. Nobody could ever see her unless she made herself known.

She scrolled through the documents on her tablet again. If their calculations were correct, then Dvorak was still somewhere in this city, as he had been ever since Y-MH-560 had been tagged. Mick had done the research, as his namesake had done a lot of logistical work when the city's foundation had first been laid. They just needed to find out where Dvorak was now, and that Gutenberg was the key. They had been slowed down by the girl's injury, but that Taggart boy was good for something -- oh, what now?

She pulled out her phone and stopped its music box melody. "*Vonces aper,* Raz?" *And it better be good, considering the time of night*, she thought.

"We've got a disturbance on the corner of 11th and

University, near where the Gutenberg was last seen," Raz said. "I've been trying to stay afloat with the authorities and make sure our records match with theirs, but the head librarian has started to suspect me in something, and she's started leaving me out of the meetings."

"You're fine where you're at," Sarah said. "Just keep being undercover at the library. We're good to have an agent like you on QWERTY. Remind me who hired you?"

"Rider did, remember? He hired me and Nikkei at the same time and assigned us to the Metro North operation for 228."

"Oh, yeah, I remember that." Sarah was quiet for a moment. "I'll get about to sending Taggart and his new...associate to 11th and University. Any clue as to what the disturbance could be?"

"Not a clue, Sarah. Not a clue in the world."

Mac had one hand on his handlebars when his phone rang. Pulling it out, he saw it was Carissa. "Hang on," he said as he slowed the bike down and stopped it on the corner of 2nd Avenue and 23rd Street. Stepping off the bike, he put the kickstand down just as Peter collapsed off of the back and sat down on the sidewalk, head in his hands.

"I am done hanging on anything for a while," he said.

Mac had to laugh. He then picked up the line. "Carissa?"

"I'm here. I got another visit from the creepy lady that I

think you should know about. She knows that you're going out to find the Bible now -- and I don't know how she knows that, but she does."

Mac nodded. Nothing surprised him anymore. "Did she say anything else? I'm kind of going in blind here, but I figured I'd start at the place where we ran into Peter last time and go from there. Then again, it's a bit vague, but I was just going to look for something apple themed."

"She gave me another piece of paper, something about the intersection of 11th and University. Does that make any sense to you?"

Mac thought in his head for a second. "It does," he said. "It's right in the area. We'll head there now. Are you still in the hospital?"

"Yeah. They're going to keep me here overnight, and then I'll be home tomorrow. They told me to keep it easy. I'll be out of school for the rest of the week…assuming the school is up and running in some form."

Mac cursed to himself. He thought back to Rue's warning. Carissa was the one who had to figure out the puzzle, but apparently he was the one being selected to bring all of the pieces to her. "You stay safe," he told her. "I mean it."

"I will. Let me know what happens."

He nodded, then remembered she wasn't here to see him do that. "I'll call you back," he said, and hung up. Then, he turned to Peter. "We gotta get back up on this bike, man."

Peter clearly didn't want to be listening. He had his head between his legs, sighing and not saying a word otherwise. "Peter, dude," Mac said as he picked up Peter's cricket bat off the ground from where he had put it, "get up."

Peter looked up at Mac. "What's the use?"

"I'll tell you what's the use! There's something weird going on in our world! Nothing is making sense, and the only clue we have right now is that Carissa needs this Bible. And if we don't get it for her..." He had to stop talking. He couldn't tell Peter either what he was fearing.

"Yeah, whatever." Peter had lost all of his enthusiasm for the project. He did stand, however, and got back on the bike when Mac directed him to. Within seconds, they were off, and Mac could tell that Peter's grip on him was looser than it had been.

"Seriously, are you okay, dude?" he asked over his shoulder.

Peter nodded. "I'm going to have to be, I assume." He tightened his grip. "Just promise you won't leave me behind. I've done you wrong by kicking you for these past few months, but if you promise me that, I won't do you wrong now."

Mac thought Peter sounded weird, but whatever. This was Peter he was thinking about, the kid who showed up at random moments with a pink slip or a notice to be there. Come to think of it, Peter had to be part of the equation. He just kept showing up at random moments like that. Was there some sort of connection?

He didn't have time to think about that right now. Right now, they had to bike, and bike they did.

They made it in record time to Union Square, passing by the shops and around the now closed park. Mac turned onto 14th Street, then University, then down to 11th Street. "I will bet you five dollars that there's something around here with an apple logo on it," he said to Peter as he slowed the bike to a halt again and both boys got off. "Stay close. We may need to get going quickly again at a moment's notice."

Peter nodded. "I'm keeping an eye out. Is there anything in particular --"

Peter never got to finish his sentence. Without warning, the bike's electric motor started up. The bike started going, hit a curb and flew through the air, hitting a nearby building. The glass windows shattered, and the people who were still sitting in the building ran for their lives.

"We need to change this," Mac said, too calm as he reached for his phone. Carissa could stop time, or even change it, if she just got her hands on an apple. Maybe Isabel could get one to her in time -- he didn't know if there were time limits on those things --

"Stop right there."

Mac turned and saw the person who had spoken to him. It was a woman, with long brown hair and the darkest brown, almost black eyes he had ever seen in his entire life. She was dressed entirely in black, but to make matters worse, she was holding a green apple in her right hand.

Mac gravitated toward her, seeing the apple. "What do you mean?"

"If you call that girl, if you get her to change this reality to what you want, then the process will just get worse for you. Accept your fate and praise God for it, for He is the one who decides who will stay and who will go. Nobody else."

Mac raised an eyebrow. "What do you mean?"

"Don't you get it, boy? I have been sent by God with an important message." Then, the woman threw the apple straight at Mac.

When the apple hit the sidewalk, it exploded in a huge ball of light that Mac couldn't see through. He heard more screaming, and then Peter's voice, frantic above it all: "Make it stop!"

Mac closed his eyes until the explosion was over. When the light faded, he opened them and found that he didn't have a scratch on him anywhere, but the area around him was destroyed. Peter was nowhere to be found.

"You already know your fate," the woman said to him without any pause. "You cannot save yourself, or the girl, or anybody. Your efforts are futile. Do not find Dvorak, or everything you know will be terminated."

Then she was gone, like a breath on the wind.

19

Welcome To Limbo

Peter opened his eyes.

He was sitting in a classroom, one that looked a lot like his. The door was closed, and the windows were foggy, with it being a winter day. His chair was in the back right corner, and he was in his school uniform. As he woke up, he looked around for his school books, but they weren't there. Neither were any of his school mates. What was this? Had he gone straight to school from Union Square? None of this was adding up. Maybe this was one of those instances where reality was messing up. Mac and his friends were talking about that, and it seemed to explain why Peter couldn't remember certain things.

None of this was adding up. And if he could just find Mac here -- or wait until school started -- then he would get his questions answered.

He stretched his legs, then rolled his neck and got up from his chair. At the very least, he should be able to go down to the cafeteria and get something to eat. But when he tried the door, it didn't open. The knob didn't have any give to it at all.

Moving around the classroom also made Peter see that it didn't seem like a real classroom at all. There weren't any signs posted on the walls, no chalk, no indication that there had been any life here at all.

Except for, Peter was now noticing, the sound of snoring.

He approached the teacher's desk with a tentative cautiousness, going back to his chair to grab his cricket bat (which had somehow made it to school with him). Then, he slowly crept toward the chair and tried to see if there was anybody in it.

There was. A young man with blonde hair and a white jacket on was sitting in the chair, dozing, arms in his lap. Peter raised an eyebrow. "What the..."

The man stirred and looked up at Peter with big blue eyes. "Oh, hello there. Wasn't quite expecting visitors yet, but you'll do. Transmissions don't come down here anyway." He straightened himself in the chair and spun around to face the teacher's desk without anything on it. "Your name, please?"

"Peter. Peter Doyle."

"Peter. Right. This makes more sense now. I am, as you can see --" and then, without any warning, a nameplate appeared on the desk. Peter leaned over to read it as the man said it -- "Mr. Michael Spowers, your teacher."

Peter gave the man a strange look. "I've never had you as my teacher before, Mr. Spowers."

"Mick. Please. This class is going to be informal enough as it is." He smiled as two notebooks appeared on the desk in front of them. "We will probably be joined here in this classroom by other students you know, as this universe decides what it's keeping and what it's chucking."

Peter raised another eyebrow. "I'm afraid I don't copy. What the smeg is going on here?"

"I'm sorry. Maybe your friends didn't fill you in. Suppose that's my job now." Mick leaned his head on his hands. "Welcome to class in limbo, Peter. The world you know and love is changing, molding as it tries to fit. And those things that get lost in the shuffle -- like you and me -- go here. In limbo."

Peter's eyes widened. "So we're in limbo? That means I'm dead?"

"You're not dead. Not yet, anyway."

"Oh. I swear, if I ever get out of here, I'm joining the drama club even though my dad told me not to." Peter paused. "If we're stuck here, we can get out, right?"

"I hope so. When the world you know completes its transformation, whatever it might be, this limbo will disappear at that time. If we are here when it disappears, then we go along with it."

Peter gulped. "So how do we get out?"

"We can't do anything. We have to wait for the girl Sarah -- my associate -- chose to decide what happens next. If she can get it straightened out, we'll go back to normal. But she only has --" Mick looked at his watch, for some reason -- "five more days to do so. And if she doesn't choose what happens to your world, then the world will start choosing at random."

Peter took a notebook and sat in the student desk across

from Mick. "You speak like you're not from my world."

Mick grinned. "That obvious, I suppose. Now, would you like me to teach you?"

Peter nodded and opened the book. "Tell me everything you know."

Mac tried to call Carissa that night.

About ten times.

It wasn't until one of the hospital nurses, a really nice lady named Jackie, picked up and told him that the hospital was closed that he quit. For the night.

He went out to his roof in Brooklyn for a while and thought to himself. Coney Island had been eerily quiet since it was winter, but especially because of the hurricane. For once, he could stay up here and think in peace, but tonight, he couldn't think about anything, save for the fact that he had tried to help Carissa...and failed.

He got up the next morning and was surprised to find that his bike was gone, left at Union Square last night as part of a police investigation. He checked the news, but there was no notice that the investigation had ever happened. Because of this, he was late to school, which was miraculously fixed, as if there had been no fire.

He decided to forget about math class -- he was ahead of everybody else, anyway -- and went up to the roof to call Carissa.

But when he got through to the hospital number, they told him that she had already been discharged. It was a sigh of relief as he hung up and then called her cell phone.

Somebody else answered. *"Diga?"*

Shoot, Mac thought to himself. It wasn't that he didn't like foreign languages, he just preferred to talk in English, as his family always had. "Is Carissa there?" he asked in English.

The tone changed. "Oh! You are the white boy, yes?"

"Yes, that's me." Mac felt embarrassed.

"Okay. I'll get her." There was a pause, and then Mac felt relieved when Carissa's voice came on the other line. "Sorry that my mom picked up the phone. She's finally started being more concerned about my health."

Mac didn't even wait. He launched into a full description of the previous night's activities, including the strange woman in the cloak. "I kept trying to call you, but they said that you were asleep," he said.

"I was," Carissa said. "That was my fault. I waited up until night hours, and then I couldn't wait anymore. This entire experience is making me very tired."

"I'll let you rest, then. I don't have my bike anymore, but can I meet you at your house after school?"

"I don't see why not. Let me just ask my mom, although I'm sure she'll let the nice white boy who rescued me in."

Mac felt his face turn three shades of red. "Okay, fine."

He got through the rest of the day just fine. During lunch, he spoke with Isabel and filled her in. "Have you seen Peter at all today?" he asked.

She shook her head. "Not at all. And trust me, I would have noticed."

They both went over to Carissa's apartment after school. The 1 line was delayed, so they took an A and walked. Carissa looked much better, and she was out of her school uniform, wearing a fitted hooded sweatshirt, green in color, and black leggings. Mac had to remind himself not to stare.

"There's got to be something special directly about that Gutenberg Bible," Carissa said as they sat in her living room and her mama brought them churros. "I was looking through my own Bible this morning, and other than heaven and hell, there's nothing about the world changing. Quite the opposite; it says that things will remain as they are, until the end of times. And I think everybody, or at least a lot more people, would be noticing if the end of the world was coming about."

"Sounds like it would be something that God, if this was true, would want people to know about," Mac said. "I'm not the most versed in Christian religion, not that I don't want to be, but it does seem like a weird coincidence that we're being asked to find out more about this Bible."

"Maybe if we go back to the library, we can at least find out more information about it," Carissa suggested. "I'm not saying we should try to find the book again -- after all, Peter is still missing. But the library may give us invaluable information on the book itself, now that we are sure it's the book and not the content we are primarily after."

They all agreed, as long as there was a Saint Arbucks run afterward at the cafe in Midtown, far from the forbidden one. Carissa got her mother's permission to go, as long as Mac was with them.

This time it was the A train that was under investigation, so they took the 1 train instead. Mac led the way down the stairs and down the elevator to the station. "It feels good to get out again," Carissa said as they got on the next train. "After being in the hospital for a day and then my house, fresh air is great."

"Yeah," Mac joked, "fresh air in a station that's so far underground that you need an elevator to get there."

"Funny."

"Hey, guys," Isabel said, "this train doesn't normally stop at Grand Central, does it?"

And Mac noticed that the car had changed. Now, they were the only ones sitting in it, and the train was no longer the old model it had once been, but the newer ones with the blue seats. There was a messaging system and electronic ride map above Carissa's head; he read it.

"We're on a 6 train," he said, in shock. "How is that even possible?"

20

The Six Train Is Too Late

"The six?" Carissa asked. "But that can't even be possible. The six runs on the east side, not the west. It doesn't make any sense."

"But it does." Mac sat down on the blue bench. "The fact of the matter is this: everything that doesn't make sense, makes sense in these strange changing pockets of madness. Reality morphs at the speed of light, without us even noticing that we're doing it."

"Oh, how right you are," a very familiar voice said. Mac and Carissa looked up to see the old lady standing in the car with an apple in her hands, as normal and expected at this point. "What do you want with us?" Mac asked.

"Uh huh," the lady said, using language that no old lady should be using. "You really expect me to believe I'm here for all of you."

She had a point. "Okay," Mac corrected, "what do you want Carissa for?"

"Oh, the usual. Giving her cryptic clues that she can't understand, because it's all I can give her." The lady paused. "Although I do have a quick question to ask of you, sir Taggart. You were out with the Doyle boy the other night looking for the book, were you not?"

Mac's eyes widened. "How did you know?"

"This is the only piece of advice I have for you: stay away from that woman in the cloak. She is nothing but trouble. Carissa, it's up to you to find that book and why it's so important."

"That's where we're headed," Carissa said. "But we don't know why the train decided it was going to be a six train instead of the one. Is it another clue?"

The old lady looked confused. Then, she looked up at the ride board and her face changed. "Okay, I didn't do that," she said and she disappeared as quickly as she had shown up on the train.

Carissa wanted to say something in the awkward silence that followed, but she didn't know what to say. "So she didn't make this the six train?" Mac finally said. "The plot thickens."

"If she didn't make this six train," Carissa said, "then who did?"

Isabel shrugged, then pulled out her phone. "You know what we should do? Take pictures. Even if they don't survive a time slip, then we can make sure we remember this train better."

Carissa nodded. "But why a six, though? I think that's our biggest clue. No matter how you slice it, we're not supposed to be on this train."

Isabel took pictures of the car, of its seats and its ride board, of the information listed on the maps, and everything else. "Get together, you two," she said, and Carissa realized she was speaking about Mac and her.

148

"Oh, us?" she asked, but it was too late. Isabel was putting them together, having Carissa sit next to Mac and putting Mac's arm around Carissa. Carissa blushed and made the mistake of looking at Mac's face, noticing it was red as well. "Are you okay?" she asked.

"Let's just take the picture and get it over with," Mac said as Isabel went to the middle of the car and held up her phone.

"Okay, guys! Look at me and say cheese!"

She sighed and punched a number into the phone. *"Vonces aper?"*

"Did you tell them about Ariana?" Raz asked.

Sarah sighed again, more of a groan this time. "I did. That crazy woman is trying to keep us from finding Dvorak. Help those guys out when they get to the library, or you're fired."

The gang arrived at the library without any trouble; their mysterious six train ran express all the way from 181st Street to Times Square, at which point it stopped running and let them off. Upon their departure, it sped off on the tracks, going who knew where.

Carissa sighed. "None of this is making any sense," she said. "But whatever. I'm not going to try and make sense of that right now. One clue at a time, and we have to figure out what's going on with the book."

They walked through Times Square and over to Bryant Park, then around to the library's entrance. There were a bunch of people sitting there, and they had to move past them and around to get through.

"Which reminds me," Mac said. "Carissa, there's a deli on the corner of Madison and 41st. It's a bit far, but I'm sure you can run there and grab an apple if we need one. We should start carrying one at all times."

Carissa nodded. "You never know when you're going to want to rewrite something."

They went back upstairs to the reading room and found that all of the tables were taken. Isabel pouted. "No fair!"

"We didn't come here to sit down and slack off," Mac said as he went up to an older black woman, another one of the librarians. "Hey, do you have any information on that Gutenberg Bible that was stolen a few days ago?"

The librarian gave Mac a strange look. "What you talking about? We got the Gutenberg right here. You can't see it, of course. You gotta need an appointment."

"Are you bothering my friends again?" a somewhat familiar voice said, and Mac turned to see the librarian named Raz there. Raz smiled at him. "You're the one who was inquiring about the Gutenberg, right?"

"Yes," Mac said, not really knowing what was going on but playing along.

Raz smiled at the other librarian. "This is our 2:00 appointment," he said, and the woman simply moved out of his way. "Go ahead and get your other friends and bring them back here," he said.

Mac made a motion to Carissa and Isabel. "This way, guys." When they got closer, he said, "Apparently we had an appointment, and none of us knew it."

"Oh, I knew you guys were coming." That was Raz as he led the three through a back door and into a separate room with the lights off. "You're assisting QWERTY right now, aren't you?"

Carissa raised an eyebrow. "What's QWERTY again? It sounds familiar, but I can't put my fingers on it."

"The creepy old lady is from QWERTY," Mac reminded Carissa. "And the girl who talked to me in the cafeteria."

"Oh."

"And so am I," Raz said, flipping on the lights and revealing what Mac, Isabel, and Carissa hadn't been expecting to see.

21

The Calm Before The Storm

Raz showed signs of resistance on his face, and rightfully so. He watched as the three human kids took a look at what appeared to be the Gutenberg Bible they had been looking for. There wasn't a page out of place, and it looked like it had never been stolen.

Or so it seemed.

"You've got to be kidding me!" Mac yelled as he ran toward the book. He then reached for it without thinking, but then realized that the book wasn't real. His hand passed straight through it. "What?"

"As you know, the real book was stolen," Raz said as he walked over to the platform where the book was normally kept. "This room is usually the only place this book is kept. It's occasionally put out for the public to see, but on normal days it's only available for private viewing, and only with a librarian in the room. It's a very rare book."

"A very rare book that is still very much stolen," Mac noted, passing his hand right through the illusion.

"That is true," Raz said. "And you are the only ones who know it. As well as me. This hologram was created by me, with the small extent of my powers that I have here, to make sure that nobody notices that the real thing is gone. To them, it looks like the real thing on the outside. And it does. But on the inside, there are some clear differences because I don't know every detail of its interior, and therefore I am not able to recreate every detail as such." Raz looked over and saw Mac and Carissa looking completely clueless. "I assume that nobody has told you anything about what I am saying."

"Yep," Mac said. Obviously Raz had hit a nerve. "Absolutely little about absolutely nothing."

"Basically this is a fake version of the book, to fool people," Raz said. "Everybody else feels and sees a real book, except for you. But the real thing is still stolen, and is still out there. You have to find it...which is why I'm curious to see why you're here when you should be looking for the book."

"We were hoping that if we came back here," Carissa said, "that we could find out more about this particular Bible. What makes it so special that we have to find it?"

"That is top secret information in QWERTY," Raz said, his arms crossed. "I can't tell anybody that, much less you."

Carissa rolled her eyes. "Then we're wasting our time with this business. If you think that I'm just supposed to find out all of this information without receiving any clues, then I won't do that."

"Are you sure?"

"Sure I'm sure. Yeah, reality's kind of messed up, but can't the old lady fix that by herself?"

Raz moved so quickly that Mac didn't even see him do it. He whisked across the floor and grabbed Carissa by the shoulders. "You realize you're on a deadline?" he asked. "And furthermore, you realize that if you don't fix reality by the fated day that everything you know will most likely be destroyed?"

"What do you think you're doing?" Mac yelled and tried to pull Raz away. "Put her down!"

"I want an answer first!" Raz yelled, then looked Carissa right in the eye.

Carissa was silent for a moment, then shook her head.

"I didn't think so," Raz said as he let go of her and put some distance between himself and her. "But I can't blame you. It's not like we've told you too much. And we can't. We can only tell you what you're allowed to know, and nothing else."

"Why not?" Mac asked.

"Because we cannot influence Carissa's decision," Raz said. "When it comes down to this universe and the decisions she must make, the puzzle she must figure out, only she can determine the best course of action. The Bible, however, has something that can help you in your search for the answers. And once you figure out the clues, you'll be able to know where to find him."

Carissa was confused. "Who?"

"Dvorak. He's one of the highest members of QWERTY. He's the only one with the power to stop all of these time issues. But we don't know where he is, and people from QWERTY can't get through to this world all the time to search for him ourselves. I myself am using all of my own world manipulating power to create the fake book in front of you. So we needed someone from your world to help us -- and Carissa is that person."

"So you're really not from this world?" Carissa asked.

Raz shook his head. "Mac, you're aware of that, aren't you? Rue filled you in on a few things, but the fact that we're not from here isn't a secret, and shouldn't be from the three of you."

Carissa wondered what other things than this mysterious Rue girl had told Mac. Who was this Rue, anyway? "So let's just say that we fail, and we don't find Dvorak," she said. "Hypothetically, because clearly you want me to find him. But what if I don't find him? All the old lady would say is 'or else.' Or else...what?"

Raz was quiet for a minute. Then, he spoke. "The world will continue to change, and then will stabilize again," he said. "But the world will not be the same. Some things will disappear forever. Carissa, since you are the chosen one, you will not disappear, but it's very possible that your friends will. It's already happened to one of your friends."

"So that's what happened to Peter!" Mac said. "You're saying he's -- he's --"

"Not dead," Raz said. "Peter is savable if Carissa finds Dvorak in time. But she must find him. Otherwise, the rest of the world will reassemble at random, and Carissa won't be able to pick and choose who stays and who goes. That's why she needs to help QWERTY find Dvorak. He has the most power to control everything, and he can bring the time slips and other issues to a stop. He can bring back Peter and make sure all of your friends do not disappear. But that will only happen if you find him -- and quick."

"Do you know when the designated day is?" Carissa asked. "I don't want it to be, like, today or something. That doesn't give us a lot of time."

"It is soon," Raz said. "Too soon. I myself don't know exactly when it is. Only my boss knows that, and Dvorak himself. But you must act quickly. Today, even."

"What would we even do today?" Isabel asked as Carissa took a phone call. "We know kind of where the book is, but Mac got beat up while trying to find it."

"Yeah, and thanks to my carelessness, both Peter and my bike are gone," Mac noted.

Raz nodded. "You may certainly work at the pace you wish," he said, "but understand that time waits for no one."

"Uh, guys..." That was Carissa, in the corner of the room, surrounded by bookshelves that created an alcove. "That was my mama. She thinks I've been out too long and wants me to come home now. What do you say we continue talking at my place about this?"

Mac and Isabel agreed and took the train with Carissa back

to Washington Heights, but didn't get a chance to elaborate any more about what Raz had told them. Her mother let them stay in the house, but wouldn't leave Carissa's side.

"You have been through enough in the last few days," she said to her. "You need to take it easy."

At least easy meant inviting Mac and Isabel to help make churros in her kitchen. Mac stirred while Isabel did the work of making sure the dough rolled the right way. "You have to make sure you keep stirring," Isabel said as Carissa came into the kitchen with plates.

"I am, I am," Mac said. "I'm trying to think at the same time. It's just hard to talk about anything, you know?"

"Talk about what?" Carissa's mother said as she came into the kitchen from the living room. The petite woman zoomed past Mac and took the bowl from him. "Not bad, not bad. Carissa, did you teach him how to stir?"

"No, Mama," Carissa said. "Maybe Isabel did --"

"Well, he's quite a cook, then! I can just tell from the way this batter looks. He'll make a great husband someday." Carissa's mother smiled while Mac just looked embarrassed.

Shyness or no shyness, the three of them finished the churros, and Mac got to take some of them home with him. "Text me when you get home," Carissa said both to Mac and Isabel, and they both did.

She took it easy that night and ate some churros, watched a

bit of television, and went to bed. The news was still covering the missing Gutenberg Bible, and there were no leads, which surprised Carissa. Couldn't the NYPD do anything? But then again, this entire situation really wasn't meant for the NYPD to begin with. She got ready and went to bed, but she couldn't sleep for the longest time. She was too busy thinking about what Raz had said earlier at the library.

"I have to find Dvorak, or everything I know could be taken away from me?" she asked herself in the dark. It was a strange question to ask, and he hadn't really elaborated, but he had seemed completely serious when he had said it. That and he had grabbed her by the shoulders to make a point.

But she knew it was also true, as well. She would do anything to make sure that the people she loved were fine. That only left one question, maybe two: where was this Dvorak person?

And what did he want?

22

Washington Heights Goes Missing

Carissa woke up the next morning to the smell of burritos. She dragged herself out of bed and made her way through the apartment.

"Morning," she muttered in English, knowing that her mother would get after her. There were times when her mother expected her to use Spanish only in the house, as a way of keeping tradition alive.

But surprisingly her mother didn't give her grief about it today. *"Buenos días, mija.* Do you want to help me bake?"

Carissa always liked making food with her mother. Her mother would tell her stories of her parents and the land they came from so long ago while they mixed ingredients like their ancestors had done. But Carissa was strangely silent today, and her mother noticed. "Are you all right, *mija?*" she asked.

She nodded. "Just stressed out. Tell me again about the chickens Abuela used to catch." And while she heard a story that she could certainly recite by heart, she zoned out and thought to herself.

Did God have anything to do with this? Sure, she went to Mass like every other good girl did, but that didn't mean she necessarily believed everything. Her mother was devout, but her father let her do what she wanted. And she wasn't a bad girl. She never stole and she did what her parents told her, and she never had any issues with people. She didn't even really hang out with guys...unless you counted Mac, whom, despite him being ridiculously white, her mother seemed to approve of.

So while she didn't see herself as a sinner, she didn't see herself as a saint either. Except that she was being treated as such by these mysterious people in QWERTY, who wanted to have her find this Bible because it had a clue in it as to where this all powerful Dvorak person was. And if she found Dvorak, then they could get Peter back and fix this whole problem. The question she really had was: why her? If God was listening and not just a tradition, then what was His plan?

"Mama always says it's not so simple," she thought to herself as they finished the burritos.

Carissa's mother let her go to the corner store to get some soda pop, and together they watched her mother's favorite telenovelas. Carissa didn't usually watch them -- they were more Isabel's cup of tea -- but if she was doing it with her mother, then it was worth it. After normal school hours, she went to go call Mac -- but instead, he called her first.

"Do you want to meet up at the Saint Arbucks in Midtown?" he asked. "The safe one that Isabel found for us, near the library. Only if you're allowed."

Carissa checked with her mother, and it was fine as long as she took her phone with her and checked in often. Carissa agreed, and took the 1 train down to Times Square without any issues. Mac was in the Saint Arbucks waiting in the back, at a table, when she arrived. When she got closer, she could see there was something else waiting for her: a chai.

"Been a while!" she said as she took it from the table and, sitting down, sipped it.

"I just got a normal one, nothing special," Mac said. "I should have asked you if you wanted it a particular way. I think you like yours with extra espresso in it."

"Oh, no, this is fine," Carissa said, suddenly flustered. She took another sip of chai to try and calm down her nerves. "As I said...been a while."

"It has," Mac said, which didn't calm Carissa down at all. She wound her legs around her chair and leaned her arms on the table, suddenly realizing that there was much less space at this table than she had anticipated. Which also meant that if she leaned forward any more, she would quite be in Mac's personal space. It was somewhere she wasn't sure she wanted to be yet.

"So," she said, now that she had her chai, "why did you call me out here?"

"Do I have to have a reason?" Mac asked. "I just figured you'd want to get out of your apartment after a long day there. I mean, I was bored all day, but then again, I was at school..."

Carissa was no longer listening to what Mac was saying. Rather, she was focused on what he was NOT saying. If he wasn't giving her a straight answer...then what was his motive? Did this involve Dvorak? Or didn't it? Did it involve her? It had to, otherwise she wouldn't be here. And Mac was here. She felt the world spinning around her and thought, for a fleeting second, that maybe the world would skip again while she sat here. But no, there were no apples. Saint Arbucks sold bananas, but they clearly weren't the same.

So were they going to talk Dvorak? Or wait, Isabel wasn't here. Was this personal? And he had bought her a chai. Was this him getting to know her better -- or even a "define the relationship" talk at the Saint Arbucks?

"Uh, Carissa? Are you okay?"

Carissa took a deep breath and sipped her chai. "Why are we here? Honestly? I need an answer before I get another headache."

"Oh, okay. I mean, I wanted to see you...but I was also trying to think of a way that we could get the Gutenberg Bible back. We know what district it's in. We just have to find a way to search the area and then get out without being caught by, I don't know, tens of thousands of people. People who are all then going to blame us for stealing the Bible when we clearly didn't. So what I was thinking was that we could stop time -- you could do it by the apple thing -- and then while everybody was frozen we could look for it in Union Square. The book seems like it's outside the effect of the time slips. Otherwise, none of us would be here right now."

Carissa nodded, her DTR thoughts long gone. This was strict business. "So you're saying that if we can just stop time for a little while we can finally get this straightened out."

"Right." Mac paused for a moment. "I just want to make sure you're okay with that. You're the one in charge of this, Carissa. You're the one who has been chosen. Whatever that means, it also means that I can't make these decisions for you."

"But I'm glad you're helping," Carissa said. "I'm not sure where I would be if it wasn't for you. Still lost and without a clue on all of this Dvorak stuff, that's for sure." She was quiet for a moment. "I know that I didn't really know you before this started..."

"I hope that we're able to stay friends," Mac said, and at the word 'friends,' something in Carissa wilted. He continued: "You've certainly brightened up my days here, and I want you to see this through. For all of us." And then he added, "And I'm not just saying that because apparently I might disappear if you don't find Dvorak. A lot of things might disappear if you don't find Dvorak, including your parents and best friend. I am committed to helping you find him in any way possible. And then, after this mess is said and done, we can still hang out. And eat your mom's churros. Seriously, those things are that good."

Carissa remembered that her mother had wanted her to call when she had gotten to Saint Arbucks. "Hang on a second," she told Mac, then pulled her phone out and dialed it. It only took a couple of seconds for her to hang up. "Okay, that's weird."

"What's weird?"

"My phone just said that my mama's number was not in service. Hang on, let me go outside where the signal is better..."

And she did. And it still didn't go through. "Can I try your phone?" Carissa asked as she went back into the Saint Arbucks.

Mac nodded and handed over his much simpler phone to her. She knew the number by heart; it had been their number for years, and her grandparents' number long before she herself had existed. But again with the "this phone number is not in service" message.

"This has me worried," Carissa said as she handed Mac's phone back to him. "Can we go home now?"

She took her chai to go as they left the Saint Arbucks, hurrying over to Times Square. They took the next 1 train headed toward Washington Heights, which arrived in the station right as they got there. Carissa sat down for a minute, exhausted, and sipped her chai as the train thundered through the tunnel. "I'll feel better once I get home and find out that my parents are okay," she said.

"I'm sure they're fine," Mac said, although he couldn't be completely sure. This was a new world, after all, one where he didn't make the rules. The girl who sat next to him did.

They made it as far up as 145th Street, and then the train

stopped running. "This is the last stop," the conductor said, and everybody else got off of the train as if it were normal.

"Excuse me," Mac said to the conductor as they got off the train, "will there be a train behind this one going to 181st? You know, one that goes to Washington Heights."

The conductor gave them a look that made Carissa's heart fall. "Where again? This train goes to Morningside Heights, not Washington Heights. There is no such place as Washington Heights."

Carissa was completely speechless, so Mac took her chai from her so it wouldn't be spilled. "What's up ahead, then?"

"The Inwood Land Preserve. Goes all the way up to the tip of Manhattan. By law no trains or buses or cars can trespass over or under it, so your best bet is to walk. It's not too far from here." With that, the conductor shut the car doors and marked the train as out of service.

"The reality slips are getting worse," Mac made notice of aloud as Carissa tried not to freak out more. She finally spoke, and it all came out at once.

"If Washington Heights doesn't exist anymore, then Isabel doesn't exist anymore! Where am I going to go? What am I going to do? Does the school still exist? Will this reset itself tomorrow? Did Mama and Papa go to the same place Peter went? We have to get them back!"

"We will. I promise." Mac had no doubt of that now.

"But..." Carissa took a deep breath. "If I can't go home now, where am I going to go?"

Mac had only one solution. "Until we figure this out, until we get your family back...you stay at my place."

23

To Coney Island

Carissa tried to form the correct words. "Your -- your house?"

"It's the only place we have to go. If Washington Heights is gone right now, then so is Isabel, and her house is ruled out too. And we can't stay at the school." Mac bit his lip. "There's really no other place, although I have to wonder..." He pulled out his own cell phone and dialed a number, then holding it up to his ear. Five seconds passed and then he smiled. "Yep. We're good. Just got my answering machine. Mom's not home yet, but that was her voice, so we're all good."

Carissa was a bit confused. "All good? Wait, we're still going to your house?"

"Yeah. My mom will be home later tonight." Mac smirked at Carissa. "What, are you afraid of being in an apartment alone with me?"

"It's not that," Carissa said, although now she was trying not to squirm. The thought of being alone with Mac for ANY period of time threatened to make her sick. But it was true; there didn't seem to be any other options. "Are you sure everything is going to be okay?" she asked.

Mac looked her right in the eye. "Don't you trust me by now?"

Carissa almost objected, but found she couldn't. Because Mac had never given her a chance to not trust him. Ever since the beginning, when she had found his note in her locker and met him on the roof, she had trusted him. They had been on their share of adventures up until now, and going with him on this next one wouldn't be any different.

Mostly.

"Your mom will definitely be back, right?" she asked.

Mac nodded. "We better get going. It'll take a while to get there, since I don't have my bike anymore."

And he was right -- the train stopped several times over the bridge to Brooklyn, and Carissa wondered if she was ever going to get there. Going at this time on a Friday meant also that they got stuck in rush hour, and she was squished between a stroller and a bass guitar. Mac had it worse; he was two people away and next to the screaming baby that always seemed to be on every train. Mac had said that they needed to take the train all the way to the end of the line, and it did seem to take forever, winding back underground and then above, stopping at each stop without warning. Carissa now knew why Mac liked having his bike on him at all times, and felt sorry for the fact that he didn't have it anymore.

Finally, the train slowed down and arrived at the terminal. Mac and Carissa had more space now and were able to easily exit the train. "I'm kind of glad the train didn't do something weird,"

Carissa said. "By now I'm used to the unexpected."

"Well, this is all according to plan," Mac said. Then, he paused. "Mostly."

"Mostly?"

"Except for the 'going to Coney Island because Washington Heights disappeared' thing."

"Oh, yeah. That." Carissa tried to laugh, but nothing came out.

"Don't be nervous," Mac said. "We just have to find this Dvorak guy, and Raz and that old lady are gonna help us. We'll get everything back to normal."

"I hope," Carissa said as Mac led the way out of the terminal and toward Coney Island. Since it was the dead of winter, all of the amusement rides were closed for now. Carissa remembered the hurricane that swept through the area in October. "Did your family do all right during Sandy?" she asked. "We were fine."

Mac nodded. "We got lucky. Our building is far enough inland that there was no structural damage. We did have to evacuate, and the basement flooded, but they pumped that out and are still in the process of reimbursing those families who lost things in the flood. Mom and I are on the fifth floor, though, so we were fine once we returned after the power came back on."

"Where did you stay?"

"Mom's boss lives in Park Slope, and he hooked us up

with a couple of friends. We crashed on couches and ate soup out of cans, but we made it." Mac cringed as he remembered something. "Oh, P.S. - the apartment's gonna be a mess. My mom's never home, just to warn you. She works at night, especially on the weekends."

"Waitress?"

"Bartender." Mac seemed surprised. "How did you know?"

"My mama used to work as a waitress in the bodega, before she went back to school and learned how to do nails. She opened up a salon with her hairdresser friends last year. But before that, she was always working odd hours. My papa was the one who worked for a long time, full time, at whatever job he could find to pay the rent, but my mama started working to help pay for my school. That's why they both work now."

They walked through the Island, past Surf Avenue and away from the amusements. "During the summers, I help out with a car mechanic in Brighton Beach, and even sometimes during the school year," Mac said as they walked. "It helps my mom with the bills. But since Sandy, the shop has been closed, waiting on federal money. That's the only way we've felt the pinch. I'm trying to be optimistic about it and do my best in school, see if that somehow translates down the road."

"Meaning..."

"Carissa, everybody at that school knows I'm smart. Really smart. And I don't know exactly what I'm going to do with it, but I'm going to go to college here in the city, on a scholarship, whatever pays for it. And then, I'm going to get a job, and my mom won't ever have to worry about paying our bills again."

Carissa was shocked to hear all of this coming from Mac. "You...you really seem like you have everything figured out."

"I try to. We're not bad off, the storm has just set us behind and caused me to really look at things. That's all. I'm sure that's just how reality goes." Mac turned to Carissa. "I'm sure you see that in your own family, as well."

Carissa nodded. "How much farther?" she asked. "It's getting chilly, and I apparently forgot my hat and gloves in another dimension now."

"Not that much farther."

They walked farther away from the ocean and up to a good sized apartment building. It looked newer than Carissa's, and much less like a former tenement house. Mac unlocked the front door and led Carissa to a small elevator which barely fit both of them. She held her breath and didn't even realize she was doing it until she got out.

"This is it," Mac said as he unlocked the door and let her in.

Truth be told, it was bigger than Carissa had been anticipating it would be. There was a living room off to the left side with clothes and papers everywhere -- in fact, it looked as if it had not been cleaned since Sandy. The kitchen wasn't much better off; in fact, Carissa was pretty sure that she smelled something coming from there.

"Don't pay any attention," Mac said as he grabbed Carissa by the arm. "We'll be in here."

He pulled her into a side room, turned on the light, and shut the door. Carissa forgot how to be nervous as she looked around the room. There was a huge television screen on one wall, along with cabinets and cabinets of DVD cases. There was a desk in one corner, a couch in front of the television, and dozens of video game consoles lying around.

"You'll be sleeping in here," Mac said as Carissa stared in shock.

"Is this...your room?" she finally asked.

He laughed. "No, this is just where I put my stuff. Mom let me have this extra room. We rented it out for a while but haven't recently, especially since Sandy. So I've been putting the extra stuff in here. My bedroom is down the hall, if you want to see it."

"No thank you," Carissa said immediately. She didn't even want to think about the fact that Mac would be sleeping in this same apartment later tonight.

Mac grabbed a remote control from the wall it had been hanging on and pointed it at the television. "Up for some TV?"

They ended up switching the channel to one of the game systems, and first Mac played against Carissa in the game that was already loaded, some dancing game where you had to step on the right colors. Then, they played a puzzle game to see who could clear the rows quickest. Mac had told Carissa he was notoriously good at the game, and yet he kept getting beat by her. "I had no idea you were good at this game!" he said with a smile after being beat for the fifteenth time.

Carissa laughed. "It's all in the wrist," she said, her anxiety long gone. She was having fun now, and even though it was just her and Mac, everything was fine. "Want to play again?"

"Hold on." Mac was quiet for a moment, then he turned off the television. "Shoot."

Carissa tried not to panic. "What's going on?"

"My mom's home early. I was hoping that you would be asleep before she got here." He went outside the room and turned to her. "Stay here and don't make any noise." With that, he shut the door.

Carissa's eyes widened. What was going on here? Mac was definitely keeping something from her. She made sure the television was off, then walked up to the door and pressed her ear to it. If Mac wasn't going to tell her, then she was just going to have to listen in.

24

Mac's Mom

Carissa couldn't hear a thing.

She wished she had a drinking glass, like in all of those television shows that depicted people being able to listen by putting a glass up against the door. But Mac's bonus room was strangely well put together and, while the gaming systems were kind of in a heap on the floor, there wasn't a dish in sight. Curses.

But she stayed patient and waited, seeing if anything would change. At least if Mac came back she would get some answers --

"Well, why didn't you just tell me?" That voice did not sound good. Carissa clenched her teeth. Was Mac not supposed to have girls over? Never mind that this was an emergency of otherworldly proportions.

Then, the door opened without any warning, and because Carissa had been leaning against it, she tumbled over and into a woman who must have been Mac's mom. She was short, with brown hair, incredibly white, and with a glazed look in her blue eyes. And in that moment, Carissa understood.

"Well, looky here!" Mac's extremely drunk mother said with a smile. "You did bring someone home!"

Carissa could hear Mac saying "It's not like that" in the background, but apparently his mother's ears weren't working at the time. She smiled at Carissa. "And she's hot, too! Look at her. Who wouldn't want to take her home! About time, too. Make yourself at home here, sugar. Do you want anything to drink?"

Carissa raised an eyebrow. Was she being objectified? By Mac's own mother? What was going on here?

"We only have water, Mom," Carissa heard Mac's voice somewhere else in the apartment.

"Nonsense," Mac's mom said again as she stepped into the game room, effectively trapping Carissa in it. "I'm sure we can find her something. What's your name? Are you a classmate?"

Carissa never got a chance to even think about asking. Mac had grabbed his mother by the shoulders and spun her around, nearly picking her up and escorting her out of the room. "I told you not to come in here," he said. "This is my room, Mom. You said so yourself."

Mac's mom turned from jovial to cross. "Oh, so you think that just because you've got your girlfriend over here means you can --" then a word Carissa didn't want to think about -- "around all you want in your extra room?"

Mac didn't say anything else. He took Carissa by the hand and pulled her aside. "Get some sleep, Mom," he said as he went out the door and out of the apartment, Carissa now behind him. Mac's mom was now screaming, but Carissa didn't pay any attention to her words. The entire situation was making her dizzy.

Before she knew it, Mac had led her up the stairs in the

apartment building and through a barricaded door with an emergency exit handle on it. The door did not ring, though, and she and Mac were on the roof, above the other buildings in the area. Carissa could see the Manhattan skyline from where she was.

She took a breath. "I have a feeling I missed something."

Mac took a breath. "So yeah, that's my mom." He gave a nervous laugh, and she gave a nervous laugh, and then they were both laughing.

"Are you sure we'll be okay?" Carissa asked.

"Yeah. Mom will rant on about this to herself for a while, and then she'll go to sleep, and I'll take you back in and lock you into the room. You've got your cell phone, so you'll just have to text me if you need to use the bathroom. My mom can be kind of..."

"I can see," Carissa interrupted. "You're sure the alarm won't go off?" she asked, referring to the door.

Mac nodded. "It never does. I come up here in the summer to think a lot. Usually too cold in the winter."

"I noticed," Carissa said, pulling her arms around herself. "Certainly gets windy up here."

"It's cold because we're high up, but we're also near the ocean." Mac touched Carissa's shoulder and moved her to the side, showing her the other view from the roof. The parks were dark, but beyond that Carissa could only see the dark, moving mass of the ocean, stretching out to the horizon line.

"Wow," Carissa said at the same time Mac said, "It's better during the day. You can actually see stuff then."

"But still, it's really cool." Carissa turned back to Mac. "So your mom works all the time?"

He nodded. "Always comes home like that, too. She's smart enough at this point that she prepares for it, makes sure she can get home in one piece, but I still worry about her. It's gotten worse lately with the troubles we've been having, since the storm. I'm afraid I'm gonna get called into the office one of these days and there will be an officer waiting for me." He was silent for a minute, then added, "I don't know what I would do without her."

Carissa finally confronted the elephant in the room -- or, in this case, on the roof. "You haven't mentioned your father."

"That's because there's no reason to." Mac took a deep breath. "I wasn't actually born in America. My mom and I emigrated from Ireland before I can remember. My father was in the military and was supposed to join us." A pause. "Of course, things don't ever go according to plan. I don't even remember him."

Carissa was silent for a moment. "I'm sorry," was all she could think to say.

"No reason to be. These things happen, and there's nothing you can do about them. Besides, he's the one who decided to be in the military. Though I wish the American government hadn't started the war that got him killed in the first place."

Carissa thought for a minute, then answered him. "Your family and mine, they're not all that different. My grandparents came from overseas looking for a better life, just like your family did. I think a lot of New Yorkers have that in common, actually. We're all from different areas of the world, but we all come together in this city."

"You're right," Mac said, and then he took out his outer jacket that he had been wearing and draped it over Carissa's shoulders.

She gave him a surprised look. "What was that for?"

"You were shivering. I'm not sure you even realized it."

"Oh." She blushed. "I'm sorry."

"Again, no need to apologize."

"I mean about the shivering."

"Oh, that. It's okay." Carissa felt her face color again. Why was she feeling this way? Was it because everybody always said stuff about her and Mac? Or did she actually feel something? She thought back to the conversation she had had with Mac back at the Saint Arbucks. Back then, she had been blowing the entire thing out of proportion...or had she been?

"Mac?" she asked, breaking their silence.

"Mmhmm?"

"Do you think...that..." She didn't know how to say anything without seeming weird. This was awkward. "I don't know. Nevermind."

It was quiet for a moment. Then, Mac spoke. "I never anticipated that any of this could have happened," he said. "But it did. I just wanted to live a quiet life in Coney Island, and then I started noticing changes. And you were the only one who saw the world I did. It's almost like fate, though. Our families are similar, and, well, you've put up with me for this long." He laughed. "I just hope that after all this ends, neither one of us disappears to wherever Peter went, or you don't end up forgetting me or something. In fact, that would rather suck."

And those words stuck out more than any others had. Carissa gave Mac a hug, then was surprised to find the hug returned. She had never properly realized how alone he had been before; she was probably his first friend in a long time. That explained why he was helping her so much; anything else was all blown out of proportion.

Until he broke the hug and kissed her on the forehead, looking into her eyes. "Just...don't forget me."

Carissa forgot how to breathe, and was sure that Mac might kiss her, until his face changed to confusion and he spoke. "Is your butt vibrating?"

"What?" Carissa asked, but realized it was her phone. She pulled it out and was incredibly relieved to see who was calling. *"¿Dios mio, dónde era?"* she asked on the phone.

"Shut up and put me on speaker," Isabel said. "I assume

you and Mac are together."

"We are," Carissa said as she pushed the speaker button. "Say hi, Mac."

"Hey, Isabel," Mac said with relief. Isabel must have stayed in the Upper West Side after school, a fact that saved her from going into limbo with the rest of Washington Heights.

Isabel's voice came out chipper. "So, have you kissed her already?"

Mac looked embarrassed as Carissa spoke. *"Dios mio, girl!"*

"I'll take that as a yes. Where are you guys? I went shopping after school and just now tried to get home. Did you cause this?"

"We didn't kiss, we're at Mac's apartment in Coney Island, and no, I didn't cause this." Carissa sighed, then turned to Mac.

She didn't even have to ask. Mac grinned. "Did I mention the couch in the extra room is a pull out couch?"

"I knew there was a reason I liked you," Carissa said to Mac, then turned back to the phone. "Isabel, I'll text you the address. Get here as quick as you can, considering it's a Friday night in the city. We need a plan to get that Bible back and stop these messes as soon as possible. I want my nabe and my parents back."

180

25
How To Save The World

"Are we ready?" Carissa asked, her cell phone in hand.

"We are ready. Over."

"Isabel, for the last time, you don't have to do that," Mac said back into Carissa's phone, which was on speaker.

Isabel's voice came out. "But it's fun, and we're on a mission anyway. Over."

Carissa rolled her eyes. "Whatever. Are we ready to go?"

"Yeah. I've got the entire Saint Arbucks on lockdown. There will be a few people in and out, I'm sure, but it's late enough that it should be fine. Over."

"Okay. We will converge on the area and I'll stop time. When everybody is frozen, we'll be able to get through and find the Bible with as much time as we need, unnoticed. Got it?"

"Sounds good. I'll stay at base. Over."

Carissa sighed. "Yeah, you're over," she joked, then hung up the phone and turned to Mac. "You ready?"

"Ready as I'll ever be," Mac said.

They were both dressed in black shirts, Carissa's taken straight from Mac's closet (and slightly big on her), and blue jeans. It wasn't the best camo wear, but for the situation it would have to do. Besides, time would be frozen in a matter of minutes anyway. Who cared what they were wearing as long as they could move around in it?

Apparently Isabel did, and she was the one who had gone to great lengths to make sure that Mac and Carissa were matching for this project. She had even taken pictures with Carissa's phone to document it, which had caused more eye rolling.

None of that mattered now, though. It was Saturday night and Mac and Carissa were ready.

When Isabel had arrived at Mac's apartment, they had kept her busy in the lobby downstairs until Mac's mother went to sleep (they didn't want to have his mom thinking that he was dating BOTH Carissa and Isabel). Post clearance, they had congregated in Mac's extra room, snacked on cheese puffs, and made the plan to get the Bible back. They didn't know what would happen next, but according to Raz, the guy from the library, it would somehow lead to the solution to their problems. They spent all of Friday preparing and decided to strike the next night.

Dvorak, Carissa thought to herself. *What a strange name for a person who can control the world. And it's unique enough. Why wouldn't we just be able to look him up on the Internet?* She was surprised that she hadn't thought of it earlier, and almost made a point of telling Mac, but then remembered that if Raz and the old lady weren't part of this world, then neither was Dvorak, which killed their chances of finding him online.

So find the Bible it was then. Carissa reached into her back pocket and pulled out the apple she had gotten from Mac's apartment this morning. It was now or never.

"What do you think you're doing?"

Carissa froze. Mac was the one who turned around, though. "You!" she heard him say, and she tried to pivot, but she was still frozen in place.

"Mac," she said, "why can't I move?"

The other voice continued. "So you do remember me." A pause, then "To be quite honest, I'm not sure you were going to."

"Where's my bike?" Mac asked. "And for that matter, where did Peter go?"

"You know where Peter went," the voice said. "And that will be where you go if you're not careful."

"What's going on?" Carissa asked. "I can't move."

"You can't move on purpose, sugar," the voice said.

Mac put his right hand on Carissa's right shoulder. "What are you doing to her?"

"Oh, just making sure that I'm not interrupted with my critical information. It's okay. I'll let you move after I'm done."

"You'll let her move now," Mac said. "She's not your toy!"

"I get to decide that," the voice continued. "She gets to decide everything else that's going on. I just think it should be fair that she knows the truth. You realize that the old lady whom you love and trust so dear hasn't told you everything, right? I bet the boy hasn't told you everything either, but you probably love and trust him more, so it's okay."

Carissa was able to turn her head to look at Mac, but no further. Mac was still visibly livid about the entire situation. "I thought I told you to put her down," he said through gritted teeth.

"Not until I say what I get to say," the voice continued. "If you want to save your world, you must not release Dvorak."

Carissa was confused. "What do you mean?" she asked.

Mac looked at Carissa. "Are you crazy?" he asked her.

"Just because she tells us something doesn't mean we have to follow or believe it," Carissa said. "Plus, if I really am the only one who holds the power, I'd like to know another viewpoint."

"You think well," the voice said, and Carissa felt the stiffness in her legs let go. She was finally able to turn around and see her assailant, a tall woman with long brown hair and a long black hood on. She immediately felt creeped out, but tried to make herself brave. Mac was here, the apple was here, and she did want to hear this person.

"My name is Ariana," the hooded figure said, "and I used to be involved with QWERTY. The old lady was my boss. QWERTY is in charge of making sure the universes operate as intended. We are all from different universes, and we are all given the power to jump from universe to universe to assist those in need. We, however, cannot change the fate of the universes we are in ourselves. Therefore, we must choose someone from that universe to temporarily give our power to and let them decide. And that is what we have done with you, Carissa."

Carissa nodded to show she understood.

"Because your universe is changing, and you and any friend you let see understand that even more now," Ariana continued. "Your universe is colliding with another as we speak, and my boss has chosen you to decide what stays and what goes in each universe. The other universe does not have this advantage. I do not know why she chose your universe instead of the other one, but she seems to favor it. This has happened millions of times before, with millions of other universes, and those without the power will never know the difference. Normally, if a guardian like yourself is not chosen, the universes collide. People, places, and things will change at random. Your friend can be here, and then the next he will be replaced with an alternate universe version of himself, and the rest of your world will have been recalibrated to fit. It's all automatic, and you will be the only one who remembers the world as it once was. But you have a chance to keep your world as it is, if you wish. Just decide it before the fated day, and when the universes collide, your world will stay the same, and the other universe will simply cease to exist."

Carissa couldn't process it. Another universe? And both of them had their fates in her hands? She had to choose one over the other, and of course she wanted to pick hers over the other to save her friends and family...but nobody in the other universe knew this danger was coming.

"Do you understand?" Ariana asked.

"I do," Carissa said, "but why doesn't the other universe have a guardian?"

"It does," Ariana said, her voice darker. "His name is Dvorak. In the instance that a guardian for the other world does not come about, Dvorak appears as an alternative to the way things have always been. And if you follow the old lady's instructions and find him and wake him up, then the world you know will be in great danger. And that's why I have to stop you from taking that book. As you probably know by now, it's the key to releasing Dvorak."

Mac sighed. "I've heard quite enough of this," he said, turning to Carissa. "What do you want to do?"

"What do you think I should do?" Carissa asked. If there was anybody she trusted, it was Mac.

Mac thought for a moment. "You want to save Peter, right?" he asked. "And your family, and your neighborhood?"

"But Mac, if she's right and there's another world out there --"

"If she's right, then this old lady friend of yours should have chosen someone for that world. The fact that she didn't means she knows it doesn't stand a fighting chance, and this world is worth keeping." Mac turned back to Ariana. "Thanks, but you're wasting our time."

Ariana growled. "You can't stop me -- even if you do stop time again!"

Carissa had had enough. She stepped forward and smiled at Ariana. "If you come with me, I'll listen," she said as she went up to the nearest storefront, a bookstore.

Ariana seemed strangely relieved. "Promise?"

"I'll do my best," Carissa said, and Ariana followed -- right through the door. As Ariana filed in, Carissa grabbed her cloak and shut it into the door, then took a bite out of her apple, and time stopped.

"She's not going to be able to move if her coat is stuck like that," she said as she returned to Mac's side. "I made sure to get her sleeve, too. We've got some time now."

"Then let's not waste it," Mac said, and they didn't. They made their way quickly across the frozen wasteland of Union Square and to 11th and University, busting down the door of each building. Nobody would see them, and this was extremely important.

It took them a while, but they found it: the Gutenberg Bible, undisturbed, in a box in the back storage room of a tea shop.

26

Zechariah 13:9

"I still can't believe we have it," Carissa said as she looked at the book. "In fact, I'm still afraid to touch it."

"You can, you know," Mac said. "And if you want to do it, today would be the day. Once this book goes back to Raz and the guys at the library, I seriously doubt they'll ever let it out of their sight again."

"If they believe this story ever happened," Isabel said as she chewed on her Saint Arbucks straw. "My guess is that nobody will, and in fact, you could probably just keep this book forever."

"Girl," Carissa said as she sipped her chai, "you have got to think this through a little bit more." *As in, we shouldn't be keeping this old book,* she thought to herself, *no matter how much you are tempted to.*

"But it's a cool book," Isabel said as she flipped through a few of the pages. "I mean, just look at it. Some of the words are even written in metallic. I didn't know they could do that a long time ago!"

"They probably melted gold to do it," Mac said as he looked at the passage in question. "What is this? Are a lot of passages like this?"

"I thought so...but now that I think about it, I think it's just that one part," Isabel said. She made sure that her fingers were clean after drinking her frapp, then flipped backward. "This one right here. It's the only passage like this."

"Maybe Isabel is going crazy because of these time slips," Carissa thought out loud. "As long as you don't stay this way, I'm cool with it. I don't ever want to lose my best friend."

"I know, I know. I'm just playing with you." Isabel pointed at the passage. "13:9, I can't read the book, though."

"Zechariah, I think." Carissa pulled out her phone and pushed a few buttons. "Here we go. *And I will bring the third part through the fire, and will refine them as silver is refined, and will try them as gold is tried: they shall call on my name, and I will hear them: I will say, It is my people: and they shall say, The Lord is my God.*"

"And in English that means...?" Mac asked.

"Sorry. That was definitely the King James translation there. That's the one my family uses for English reasons...which isn't often."

"It means that God will give us hardships," Isabel suddenly spoke up, "and then we will call him God and we will be his people."

Carissa raised her eyebrows. "Since when have you become the expert on everything biblical?"

"I don't know. I pay attention when we go to Mass every week. I think it's kind of interesting. You know how when you get bored, you're always texting people and checking your phone?

My mama takes away my phone during Mass and won't let me talk, so I don't have a lot of things to keep me busy. So, I think about what the passages could mean in real world English. It kind of passes the time, don't you think?"

"You're still crazy, but at least it's something we can use," Carissa said with a smile. Then, her smile faded. "Wait. Those are the only words in gold, right? That might be a clue to how we can find Dvorak. Does anybody know where a gold refinery is in the city?"

"No, but maybe we can go to 47th and see if Diamond Alley has any clues," Isabel said. "Can I get another drink?"

"Suit yourself, but I'm not paying for this one," Carissa said. "We've been here fifteen minutes, time is still frozen, and I'm lucky that I was able to get these two drinks the way I was."

"You manipulated the baristas into giving us those drinks," Mac said with a creeped out look on his face. "I was the one who insisted that we put money down for them."

"Yeah, yeah, whatever," Carissa said. "So I'm getting good with the time slip thing. So what." She rested her head on her hand.

Mac did the same and looked at her. "You're not still thinking about what Ariana said, are you?"

"Of course I am. All of those other people in that universe, those other versions of us that Ariana talked about...if I choose this world like they want me to do, then all of them will just..."

"You don't know that she was telling the truth," Mac said. "We can't trust her."

"Can we?" Carissa looked into Mac's eyes. "The old lady hasn't exactly been forthcoming about information."

"But Raz didn't seem like he would hurt us," Mac said. "And if we don't find Dvorak, then who knows what will happen to our world? To your family?"

Carissa couldn't think about it anymore. She simply leaned forward, to her right, and onto Mac's shoulder. Within seconds, two things happened: Mac's face lit up, and time mysteriously restarted. The people around the three friends started moving again, and the outside sounds started up.

Carissa jumped in surprise, away from Mac and back on her own chair. "What was that?"

"You started up time again." Isabel sipped what was left of her drink, giving slurping sounds. "Darn. I was wanting to get another free drink."

"Those drinks weren't free." Carissa got up from her chair. "We have to get out of here. Ariana is going to find us."

They got out of the Saint Arbucks and into the nearby subway. Since they were on the west side, at the secret Saint Arbucks by the library, Carissa suggested that they go to the east side to get away from the library itself, and they took the shuttle train over to Grand Central Terminal. They didn't have time to look up at any of the beautiful architecture or the ceiling with all of the stars.

"Hey," Carissa said, "I just remembered something. You remember when we all rode that strange train on the 1 line the other day? When the old lady was riding with us and she was confused? What train was it pretending to be?"

"A six, I think," Mac said as they moved around the corner and into a Hudson News store.

Isabel whipped out her phone and looked at it. "Here," she said. "It's definitely a six train. See?" She showed Carissa, and sure enough, there was the six train logo at the top of the train.

"Isabel, you are a genius for taking these pictures," Mac said with a smile. "Remind me to treat you to coffee when all this is said and done."

Isabel beamed. "Of course!"

Carissa tried not to be too sour about the situation. "What about me?"

Mac pulled her aside by the shoulder. "I was thinking more than coffee," he said, and then he was gone, heading toward the six train. Carissa shrugged and pulled out her own MetroCard, trying to ignore the beating of her heart.

Isabel couldn't, though. "You liiiiiike him," she said as they took the escalator down and swiped their way into fare control.

"So what?" Carissa said. "We have more important things to do right now."

Isabel's smile spread across her face. "I knew it! Wait until I tell your mother." She took out the phone as they went down the stairs and caught the six train right behind Mac. He was staring straight ahead, not talking to either of them.

"Weird," Carissa said to herself as she looked up at the ride board. "Hey, Isabel...did you take a picture of the ride board in that six train?"

"Of course I did. Why?"

"Do all of the stops match?"

Isabel looked at her phone, then back at the ride board. "There's no City Hall stop on this one," she said. "In this train, there's a stop called Brooklyn Bridge -- City Hall. But in the photo, there are two stops, one named Brooklyn Bridge and one named City Hall."

"They had those separate a long time ago, but they closed the City Hall station," Mac said. "They apparently still use it as a turnaround for six trains. Don't ask how I know that."

Carissa took a deep breath. "Guys, I think we might know where Dvorak is."

They took the train all the way down to Brooklyn Bridge. The doors opened and everybody stepped out. A conductor came over to them. "Are you planning on going uptown on this train?" he asked.

Mac nodded. "We are."

"Then please come to the first car." And the conductor led

them through the cars, all the way to the front one. There, Mac, Carissa, and Isabel sat down. With one last message and the signal, the conductor closed the doors. Then, the train started up again. It went past the last stop on the line and went slow for a few minutes, and then suddenly came to a stop. The doors opened, and Carissa knew they were here.

She made sure she had the Bible with her, then stepped out of the train. Mac and Isabel followed her. The station was creepy, dark, and the six train they had come on disappeared behind them, intent on starting its trip over on the uptown side.

"Well, this just got us a quiet, abandoned subway station," Mac said. "This is great and all, but...we don't have a way to get out of here. And even if Dvorak is here, we don't know where to find him."

"I think I know what to do." Taking the Bible out, Carissa turned to Zechariah 13:9 and started to read the passage in its native Latin. Her voice echoed out into the cavern, and Carissa noted that the ceilings must be high telling by the way it echoed. When she was finished reading the passage out loud, the letters started to glow and then disappeared.

Then, the subway station was filled with light, and they were surprised at what they saw.

27

Enter Dvorak

The room before the three continued to glow, and Carissa could look up and see the stained glass above her head. How long had that been there? This looked more like a church than any subway station she had ever seen in her entire life...which probably explained why they had needed the Bible to get in. Perhaps this was a place that, like all of the time slips, existed outside the regular time line. Maybe this place only existed here and now, instead of the real station that would be covered in graffiti and old and smelly.

This, though...this was...strange. A shrine. Still very much a station, with gates and the yellow line and staircases seemingly leading to the world above. But in the center of the platform, there was a glowing light materializing in midair, and Carissa didn't need anybody to tell her what it was.

When the light faded, Carissa realized that she was looking at a tall man wearing a suit, with jet black hair and steely grey eyes. He looked right at her and smiled. "I assume that you are the one that they have chosen?" he asked her.

Carissa figured he was speaking of QWERTY. "I am," she said. "And I have woken you up just as they have requested."

"Perfect." Dvorak looked around the hall. "So, this is the place where I woke up? It certainly seems fitting enough for someone as myself. I personally would have liked the ceilings to be a bit higher, maybe bring a bit more light in." He gave Carissa another once over. "Is it true that you have been sent from those who wish to save this world?" Dvorak asked.

Carissa shrugged. She didn't really know what he was talking about, so she could only tell the truth. "Well, QWERTY sent me," she said. "Raz and that really old lady. I don't know if you know her or not."

"A girl named Rue as well," Mac spoke up from the back.

"Silence!" Dvorak glared at Mac. "I speak only with the guardian, none other, unless it is necessary. Is that right, Macardle?"

Mac's eyes widened at the realization that Dvorak knew his name without asking. "Yes, sir."

"Now..." Dvorak stayed where he was, but crossed his arms over his chest. "Where were we? Ahh, yes. Miss Carissa Lopez, the savior of this world, as picked by my so called associates. Did they tell you anything about me?"

"I..." Carissa shook her head. "They didn't really say anything, other than we needed to find you, and you would fix everything once we did."

"Ariana said some stuff," Isabel said, then spoke again when Dvorak gave her a nasty look, "I'm just telling the truth!"

Dvorak turned back to Carissa. "Is it true that Ariana spoke to you about me?"

"Yes."

"You are aware that she is no longer a member of
QWERTY, and that she has been expelled from their ranks for
some time now."

"I didn't know all of that exactly, but I'm somewhat
aware."

Dvorak nodded. "I am one of the Lord's creator angels.
Because He has given me this great power with which to serve
Him, I decide who stays and who goes. QWERTY assists with
this, certainly, but I have the final say. And, of course, they pick a
guardian of one of the worlds, the one they feel has the most
potential. Which means that they think that this world has the
most potential. The question is...do you see it the same way, dear
Carissa?"

Carissa nodded. "In a way, I do. If there is another world, I
would feel bad about choosing our world over theirs. But this
world has my friends, and my family and my neighborhood if I
can ever get them back. And I want to, trust me. They're what is
most important to me. That's also why these two people are
behind me here. They have helped me out the entire way during
this entire journey, and now that I am here, I wouldn't have
anybody else by my side."

"Understandable. But you realize that you have to decide
which world stays and which world goes by yourself. So your
friends cannot mean anything to you while you decide."

Carissa took a deep breath. "In that case, I still choose this world...because the old lady picked it."

Dvorak nodded. "Then you realize that I do not choose this world."

Carissa raised her eyebrows. "Okay...but I choose this one. You're the one with the power, and so you can fix everything and keep this world and not keep the other one. I think this was the puzzle that the old lady wanted me to figure out, and if she put her faith in me, then I have to protect my own world. And you'll show me how to, won't you?"

"You don't even know the other world," Dvorak said, and the stained glass ceilings shattered above their heads. Carissa put her arms up to try and shield herself. This was not going as planned.

The glass evaporated into thin air before it could reach the ground. "You don't even realize what you are doing," Dvorak said out loud, his voice louder now than it had been before. "Is this just a game to you?"

Carissa remembered what Ariana had said about Dvorak...that, if given the chance, he would defend the other world because he had to. Perhaps if Carissa could prove that this world is better, then she could make Dvorak see. Perhaps this was the true challenge.

"This world is better than you could ever imagine," she said. "Sure, I don't know the other world, so I can't make a perfect comparison. But I know that this is a world where anything is possible, where people are in control of their own destinies. That's what our country was founded on."

"This country? This country?" Whatever Carissa had said had made Dvorak livid. "What does that mean?"

Carissa found her confidence shaken. "Um...well...my family came from another country a long time ago. They came here looking for a better life."

"A better life? There is no such thing. There is only the will of God, and the way He decides to execute it. And the guardians that are chosen -- those prophets who get to see His will before their world ends -- can only sit back as Jeremiah of old and watch as it all falls apart. You will wake to see another day, but neither of your friends will." Then, Dvorak turned and acknowledged Mac. "Isn't that right, Macardle?"

"That's the second time you've mentioned me by that name," Mac said with a growl.

"Oh, and you wish I would quit? Maybe because it's not your real name. Maybe because you don't have a name at all."

Carissa looked at Mac. "What is he talking about?" she asked, figuring that Dvorak was just spouting some more nonsense about something or another. But Mac had a sad look in his eyes, and Carissa got a sinking feeling in her stomach.

"Oh," Dvorak said with a laugh in his voice, "he didn't tell you the truth?"

Carissa couldn't keep her eyes off of Mac. "What did you do?"

Mac couldn't answer. He only mouthed an "I'm sorry."

"Oh, I can tell you the answer to that," Dvorak said. "Our little flaw in the system can't answer for himself anymore. Because that's what happens to people who are selfish, who break the rules. And don't say you did it for your mother, because that's not true at all. You did it for yourself, and look where it has gotten you."

Carissa wished desperately that she had an apple to try and erase this entire scene. What had she done? "You haven't told me what he did," she said.

"You must follow the commandments to ensure that the universe lives on," Dvorak said. "You must comply with the way things are. If you break the rules, you should be eliminated. And that is precisely what Macardle Taggart has done. Thou shalt not steal, yet he has stolen a number from the dead. Thou shalt not steal, yet he had masqueraded as this person for years, ever since he arrived on this shore so long ago. He will tell you that it's not his fault, but it is. And it is the way he has illegally been in this country for years now."

Carissa's mind blanked out. Mac? Illegal? "That can't be right."

"Oh, but it is. Neither him nor his sad excuse for a mother are citizens, though the fake Mac with the fake identification number has posed as one for years. An anomaly. An outlier. Someone who doesn't belong." Dvorak held up his hand. "And as such, someone who should be eliminated."

"But --" Carissa tried to talk, but it was too late. There was no flash of light, no sound effects. There was only Mac there one second, and then the next, he was gone, completely vanished into thin air. It didn't register in Carissa's mind at first, but when it finally did, she couldn't even find the voice to scream.

"Every anomaly should be eliminated from this world," Dvorak announced, his big booming voice now echoing out throughout the cavern. "And then, it will be replaced with the correct form from the other universe. In this way, I will create a perfect world in which the best of the best will survive, and you, Carissa, will have the privilege of watching me do it, as so many before you have watched. You will be a citizen of this world, this good and pleasing and perfect world for our Lord and Savior."

"You can't do this," Isabel said from the back, finally free to talk and putting on her best save the world face.

"Oh, but I can, because by freeing me, Carissa has forfeited her power to do so. From now on, I hold all of the power and will be making the decisions for this world. Your assistance will no longer be needed." And with that, much like Mac had, Dvorak simply vanished, and Carissa finally found the strength to cry.

28

The Misshaping Of Midtown

The boat was rough, and Carissa held on tight to the mast. She could smell the fresh sea air as the boat made its way to shore for the first time in days. There were hundreds of people around her, looking at the same area she was. It took a moment, but she finally recognized Lady Liberty in the harbor.

Carissa hadn't even known that she had fallen asleep until Isabel roused her, shaking her from her Ellis Island dream. She opened her eyes and found that she was lying on hard ground. Isabel was sitting by her side, her eyes on her friend. "Are you okay?" she asked.

Carissa nodded until it all came back to her -- the way Dvorak had acted, Mac's secret, him disappearing to who knew where. Then she started to shake. "I don't know."

Isabel hugged her friend tight. "You'll be okay. You always will be."

"I know, but now what? I did something really bad, Isabel, and I didn't even know I was doing it. I was just following the rules. I just did what they told me to do, and now look what happened to Mac." She sat up on the ground, trying to get her bearings back.

"Do you think that Mac..." Isabel went quiet.

"Stole somebody else's identity? I don't know. But if

Dvorak is all about the rules, then Mac broke a huge one. It's tricky. On one hand, maybe he needed to do it so that he could stay in the country. But he should have done it legally." Carissa sighed. "I can't believe I'm not needed anymore. Dvorak is here, and he's going to fix the world just like the old lady said he would. But it's going all wrong. At this point, I'm going to lose you as well, Isabel."

Isabel was quiet, then looked up at the ceiling. Carissa's eyes looked up as well, and she could see where the stained glass ceilings had been, now broken and gone.

"This entire thing is surreal," she said.

Isabel sighed. "Well, that old lady wanted you to find Dvorak, right? Why don't you just go ask her what you should do next?"

Carissa's eyes widened. "That's a brilliant idea!" she said.

"If we go to the Saint Arbucks near the school, hopefully she'll know we're looking for her."

"Hopefully Dvorak won't know," Carissa said. "Isabel, you've got a great idea. But I think we should also try to find Ariana as well. There were some things that she said that were right, and if the rest of the things she said were right, then I think she might have the best game plan as to how to stop Dvorak. We got ourselves into this mess. We need to get ourselves out." She stood up. "I wish Mac was here."

"So he could make sure everything goes according to

plan?" Isabel asked.

Carissa shook her head. "No...I just miss him." She sighed. "I hope he's gone to that same place that Peter has gone. If we can somehow get all of that back and prevent Dvorak from destroying everything..." She shook her head again, this time to clear it. "First things first. Isabel, you go uptown to Saint Arbucks and try to find the old lady. We need her help most definitely, but I want to try to find Ariana. I think she'll be around Union Square. Besides, I don't want to set anything off by going in that Saint Arbucks. That's why you have to find her."

"Sounds good. But why are you going to Union Square?" Isabel asked.

"Ariana will know by now that we released Dvorak," Carissa said. "And if she knows that, she's going to want to be in a location where I can find her so she, at the least, can say 'I told you so.' But I did want to believe her. We have to try."

"Good plan," Isabel said, "but how do we get out of here? There's no other trains."

"Oh." Carissa thought to herself for a moment. "I don't know if we could go up through the roof or not --"

Before she had even finished saying the words, the world around them had moved, and Carissa and Isabel were up and out of the subway station and on the surface. The sky was now pitch black dark, not a star in the sky, but each building glowed, and Carissa could see the nearby Brooklyn Bridge glowing as well.

When she really focused on the sky, she could see that there were cracks running through it, as if the entire world really was ending.

"How did I do that?" she asked, trying to hold herself together.

Isabel shrugged. "I don't know. But do it again. We need to split up and find the lady and your friend who told you the truth. I'll go uptown. You go to Union Square to find her, and then meet me at Saint Arbucks, okay?" She gave Carissa a hug. "I love you. Be safe, my spirit sister. Remember that I would do anything for you."

"I know, I know, stop getting so sentimental," Carissa said. "I'll be there in a short time and we'll both get chai."

"Sounds good. Now, can you beam me up to Columbus Circle?"

What am I supposed to do? Carissa thought to herself. But she put her hands out in front of her, and without any warning, Isabel disappeared with a "pop!" into thin air. Carissa sighed. "I hope she made it."

Maybe it's possible that my powers didn't disappear when Dvorak took over, Carissa thought to herself. *Far from it. Maybe they actually increased.*

She started to run, the world frozen around her, buildings glitching and water still and the air stale. With every step, the world altered itself a little bit more, but Carissa wouldn't let it faze her. *I just have to find Ariana,* she told herself. *If I can do that, then I can get the real answers.*

When she got to Union Square, which took much less time than she thought it would, the entire area had already been eradicated. The park was completely gone, replaced by a huge black hole, sucking up everything around it. Carissa wondered if the black hole was going to lead to limbo, but she didn't want to test that theory.

"Ariana?" she called out. "Ariana, are you here somewhere?" No answer. Carissa knew she needed to move on.

Isabel found herself standing in front of a very familiar looking Saint Arbucks. The logo had turned green instead of red, and there was a mermaid as a logo instead of the usual centaur, so Isabel knew the entire world was being messed with.

She went inside the café, but time stayed still. People were frozen, getting their drinks and sitting and chatting with others, their mouths frozen open. It made Isabel thirsty, but now was not a time for coffee. She scanned the café, but there was no sign of the old lady, her tracksuit, or any apples.

"Hey!" she yelled, at the top of her lungs. "If time is frozen, then you can still hear me, right, old lady? You've got to help me! Carissa's trying to save the world, and she found that herald guy like you told her to, but nothing is going according to plan and the world is being destroyed! I don't know what to do and Carissa doesn't know what to do and Mac is gone and aren't you supposed to help us?" She sighed. "Carissa would be here, but she didn't want to screw things up. She's going to see that Ariana person and get some answers. I just want everything fixed, and I want my best friend to be fine. I hate seeing her like this."

"You've got a lot of spunk coming here, kid."

The voice sounded familiar, and Isabel turned, but she did not see the old lady. There was instead a younger woman there, with a black short sleeved military jacket on. She was at a table and had a frapp in her hands, and a red apple on the table.

"But now that you're here, and now that Carissa understands, we might just have enough time to pull this off," Sarah told Isabel. "Shall we initiate the survival tactics?"

Carissa started to head toward the upper west side and the Saint Arbucks that she had sent Isabel to. Madison Square Park was empty as well, but this one was a barren wasteland instead of a black hole. Herald Square glowed so bright that Carissa could barely see. She walked around the frozen cars and people who had been passing by, still on their cell phones, pushing strollers, everybody going where they needed to go. She was the only one in this entire universe who could truly see what was going on, and she was definitely the only person who could do something about it.

Times Square, unlike the rest of the buildings, was completely dark. When Carissa got there, she could literally not see a thing. She looked around, tugging at the bottom of her shirt nervously, realizing for the first time that while it should be cold out, she didn't feel a thing. Was this how the end of the world always went? Was it always this horrible and miserable for those who were chosen? Dvorak said that he had ended worlds several times before. Had he ever been stopped? Could he be, now that he had been freed?

"Well, look who we have here."

Carissa knew that voice. She was able to see Ariana, glowing with light at the top of the stairs on 47th Street, in the middle of two flagpoles, two Old Glories frozen in place. She came down from her perch and faced Carissa. "You did it again, guardian. You didn't listen."

"And I'm sorry," Carissa said. "For everything. Is there any way to stop this? Or are we doomed?"

Ariana almost seemed surprised for a moment. "You think there's still a way to save your world? The fated day is tomorrow. Dvorak cannot be stopped."

Tomorrow? Nobody had ever told her that! Carissa held on to her shirt to keep from falling over. "It can't be."

"Oh, but it is." Ariana smiled. "You are just one in line of several living beings from several planets that have made this decision. Congrats. I hope you like your new world."

Carissa shook her head. "There has to be some way to reverse everything that has happened. Dvorak -- he's the one who created everything, right?"

"Dvorak does not create," Ariana said. "He only destroys. He breaks apart the framework, and at midnight after the fated day, everything that is broken will disappear forever."

Carissa had to think for a moment. "Including limbo?"

"Including limbo."

She had an idea. "So, in theory, if we put Dvorak in limbo and made him stay there, and the fated day happened, Dvorak would disappear forever?"

Ariana smiled. "You are the first person ever to understand that. Is that your plan?"

"Sounds like it would be, but how do we get him into limbo? I know Isabel went to Saint Arbucks to find the old lady and get her help. Does she know how? Isn't she, like, the head boss of QWERTY or something?"

There was an understanding in Ariana's eyes. "So that's how it will go," she said with a smile. "I have enough power to send you to limbo. You have to go there, gather all of your friends together, and then form a plan. Are any QWERTY associates in limbo?"

"Maybe this one person that the old lady knew," Carissa said. "He disappeared at the very start of this." As if by magic, the photograph of the old lady and the man appeared in Carissa's hands. She showed Ariana. "Him."

"Oh, so you did get that photograph!" Ariana said with a

smile.

Carissa seemed confused. "You were the one who gave us that picture?"

"Of course I did! Didn't you read the message on the back?"

"You mean this smudge?" Carissa said, pointing to the area on the back of the photo.

Ariana took one look and rolled her eyes. "That one. Sorry, I've only been trying to stop you from finding Dvorak since this entire thing began two weeks ago. At least then your world would stand a better chance. Dvorak is the only one who can make permanent changes in these realms, so if you don't contact him, your world will reassemble at random, the way God intends it. Technically Dvorak should fix the world according to your wishes, but instead he just destroys everything every time he's woken up. That's how these universe colliding things go – either the two worlds merge at random, or you wake up Dvorak thinking you can get him on your side and your world is destroyed as a result."

"Or we put Dvorak in limbo," Carissa noted.

There seemed to be a look of recognition on Ariana's face. "You said this guy in the photo, Mick, could be in limbo. That's excellent." Ariana turned to Carissa. "You need to go to limbo and talk to him. He can help you. You'll have to do it quickly, as time in limbo is the same as time in the real world. Tell him you are initiating Operation Colemak. We've never done it before, but Mick's a pro. He remembers everything. Complete Operation Colemak as quickly as you can. I will initiate the real world section of Operation Colemak here, and it should get you out of limbo and Dvorak in if all goes well. But this is the part where it is really up to you. Dvorak cannot go into limbo by himself. You must complete Operation Colemak, and by yourself. Trust me. If you do this, I will get you and your friends back out of limbo. I am sensing that it is God's will to." Ariana took a deep breath. "Are you ready?"

Carissa shouldered her white duffel, which held the Gutenberg Bible inside. "Ready as I'll ever be."

29

Operation Colemak

She didn't even notice the change. Like most things in this strange, new world, there was no notice. One minute she was in her normal world, and the next, she was standing in her English classroom, duffel still on her shoulders.

"...and that's how Equestria was formed," a voice was saying from the other side of the room. When the light faded, Carissa could see that it was a younger version of the man in the photo. This must be the Mick that Ariana had spoken of.

He stopped speaking and looked at Carissa. "What are you doing here?"

"I have been sent by Ariana," Carissa said. "She said we need to initiate Operation Colemak."

The look on Mick's face changed from shock to surprise to wonder. "Well," he said with a smile. "She wouldn't have sent you here if Colemak was impossible. I'm Mick, and you must be the guardian Sarah chose."

"Carissa Lopez," Carissa said as she stepped forward and shook Mick's hand. He was very professional, with very light blonde hair and a suit on, much like Dvorak's but with a very personable demeanor.

Mick nodded. "Sarah chose well," he said. "You figured it out."

"What is this Operation Colemak?" Carissa asked.

"I can't give you details," Mick said. "But it happens on both sides of the universe melting phenomenon -- both in your world and in limbo. If the other world has a guardian, both guardians are supposed to meet in limbo and do it, but that has never happened before in our quadrant. I take it you understand that Dvorak is the substitute guardian to the other world?"

Carissa nodded. "So why would the old lady have me find him?"

"Because his presence is necessary in order to facilitate the move, no matter what happens. Each world must have a guardian. If one doesn't, and Dvorak is not wakened, the worlds will mix at random and chaos will occur. It is not unheard of for both universes to disappear when this happens. But once there are two guardians, or Dvorak is woken up, there is balance. And if the guardian or guardians can come to limbo, then we can initiate Operation Colemak, the way to save your world. As the guardian, Carissa, you have the ability to change your world, and nowhere is that more evident than in limbo. Dvorak can cause havoc, but if you can rewrite the rules and make it back to your world in time, you will be the first and only to put an end to Dvorak." Mick sighed. "Which has needed to happen for some time now. He's gotten too arrogant about the saving worlds thing. When you eliminate him, someone else will be chosen from QWERTY's ranks to replace him, someone who will hopefully be better at their job than him. So you're not only saving your world right now: you are saving a lot of future worlds as well."

Mick sat down at his huge teacher's desk and pulled out a notebook and a pen. "I cannot tell you how Operation Colemak works in the real world," he said, "but I can tell you how it works here in limbo. Your job, Carissa Lopez, is to rewrite your world...literally. Write down everything you want to be true about your world using this pen and paper. If you can make your way back to your world, then your notebook will take effect, making everything written in it the new truth for this world. And while you are the only one who can write it, there are certainly those who want to give you support."

The door opened to the classroom, and a very relieved Mac stepped in. "I am so glad to see you," he said as Carissa sprinted into his arms.

"I am glad to see you!" she said. "You owe me some serious chai when we're done with this. You can't make me scared like that --"

She couldn't speak any more, because Mac had dipped her and pressed his lips to hers. Her eyes widened and before she knew it, the kiss was done and she was back on her feet again.

"We'll talk after this," he said as Carissa's mother and father came in, and Mac was forgotten for a moment. They conversed quickly, and Carissa's parents revealed that Mick had told them everything. Peter later came in, giving Carissa her pen and paper.

"Time is running out," he said. "Write."

And so she wrote. She wrote that she and her friends and everybody in limbo would make it safely to the real world again. She wrote that Dvorak would be sent to limbo, and after he was sent there, nobody who went to limbo could escape ever. "There will be a new limbo for each universe, right?" she asked. "I want to make sure I'm defining this limbo and not every single one."

"Correct," Mick said.

Carissa went on to write that, physically, the world should be the exact same as it was before January 6th, when the world started to change. All people should be the same, and not replaced with counterparts from the other world that was colliding with theirs. She wrote that if there were any particular individuals who were important enough to the other world that would get erased, they should instead be transported to QWERTY's operating dimension.

"If they have the qualifications," Mick said, "we would love to give them a second chance as QWERTY operatives. This actually happens frequently. If someone qualified gets stuck in limbo, we can usually rescue just that person and draft them in."

Carissa continued to write, giving every single detail she could think of. Mac held her other hand and her parents sat by her, Peter and Mick nearby. She wrote throughout the night, filling up the entire notebook, taking an occasional break to rest her hand.

She wrote of many things being the same, but also of small peaces that could be added to the world. She thought long and hard about what could be changed for the better. She added more love, more justice, inherently learned in each person. She added more wildflowers to the city parks. She made people want to drink more water and less sugar, while still giving them free will. She rewrote the role of politicians to, at least, be more open to those they represented, and she taught all how to reduce, reuse, and recycle. She connected all to the Internet and installed wireless towers everywhere, then extended the range of the signal so there would be less towers. She put a compost plant in every city that had a trash dump. She made every school have the technology and the grants to give each further generation a chance.

She changed the laws in every state in America to treat every person the same, giving religious institutions the chance to opt out. She declared an international day of peace on September 11th.

She wrote that the warring states in the Middle East should find peace and come to a solution within three years, a decision of their own but with a timeline to stop the suffering once and for all. She wrote that those who suffered from hurricanes and earthquakes would all immediately get the care and help they needed. All countries that were hungry would experience good crop years in the future, and those communities that had been hated and prejudiced against would now be internationally loved.

But she did not completely eliminate poverty, or pain, or high fructose corn syrup. There were things that she felt the world itself could decide better than her.

"I'm not sure how this is going to work," Carissa said.

"Well," Mick said, "some resources will come from the other world. Things like wildflowers and water. The love, however, comes straight from you."

Carissa nodded. "Okay, I think I got everything. Now what do we do?"

"We wait and see if Ariana is able to make the other side of the plan happen," Mick said. "She'll make it, but it will probably be down to the wire. Nobody knows what time it is, since there's no clock here."

"Yeah, and my phone is dead," Carissa said.

"Which means as long as we are existing here, it's not too late," Mick said. "We just have to have faith --"

Without warning, the classroom split open, and the room was filled with a bright white light. Carissa found herself alone again, only holding on to the book she had written her vendetta in. She found herself floating upward. Was this it? Did Ariana do it? Or was everything falling apart now? Would she disappear soon? There were no more people, no more walls, only the invisible floor under her feet.

"Carissa?"

She knew that voice -- and there she was, floating toward

her spirit sister in the light. Carissa smiled as she embraced Isabel. "What are you doing here? Did you find the old lady?"

"Oh, no you don't!"

Carissa knew that voice as well – and saw Dvorak, still in his suit, brows furrowed as he came right toward them. There was a knowing in his grey eyes that told Carissa he knew what was happening.

"Isabel," Carissa whispered, "behind you."

But Isabel made no motion to look. She just smiled. "Promise me you'll date Mac, okay? And that you'll drink lots of chai."

"What are you talking about?" Carissa asked, worry filling her voice. Dvorak was falling closer, arms outstretched, screaming at them, about ready to crash into both girls. "Isabel, we have to move!"

But Isabel simply held Carissa in the light. And with an "I'm sorry," the light faded as if it had never existed, and Carissa found herself sitting where it had all began -- Saint Arbucks, after hours. The clock on the wall read midnight exactly. Isabel, Dvorak, and limbo were gone, but the notebook was in her hands.

She looked around the cafe. Mac was sitting on the floor, near her parents, and they looked like they had all fallen quite a long distance. Peter was on top of the counter, also getting his bearings. Still no Isabel.

Mick was in the corner, locked in a deep embrace with a

young woman Carissa had never seen before. Except she had. When the woman pulled away, Carissa could see that it was the old lady, just as she had looked in the photograph they had found. The old lady looked at Carissa with a smile.

Carissa knew that smile -- it meant that they had won. Nothing made sense just yet, but they had won. That was the most important thing. "Thank you."

"No. Thank you." She even sounded younger, but it was the same lady. "You're the one we should be thanking."

"I gotta thank Isabel, actually...I saw her in the light. And Dvorak was there, coming straight for us. Where did they go?"

The old lady's smile faded, and she only shook her head.

30

It All Begins Again

They left the Saint Arbucks -- as it was technically closed -- and went over to Columbus Circle. The night was now normal, and busy as New York always was. The old lady -- or who used to be the old lady -- cleared her throat. "I assume Mick caught you all up on Carissa and her role in all of this?"

Everybody nodded.

"Well, when Carissa left our world for limbo, as she had to do in order to initiate Operation Colemak, she left a void in this world. There was no longer a guardian in this realm. And so, a new one had to be chosen."

Carissa could see where this was going. "You mean..."

"I was sitting at the Saint Arbucks when your friend came in," the lady explained. "She was scared but intent on finding me, as evidenced by the way she was making a scene. She asked if there was any way we could stop Dvorak. I told her there was only one possible way we could, and then Ariana arrived and said that they had initiated Operation Colemak. In order to keep the power equal, and to not let Dvorak get an advantage in our world, I made Isabel the new guardian. The guardians have the power to create whatever they want to in limbo, and Operation Colemak usually works by both guardians coming together in that limbo. That's why Carissa had to go to limbo to rewrite the world. Isabel became a guardian who could also rewrite this world, but Isabel only had one wish: that Carissa's notebook, and every request in it, take hold in this universe."

"Wow," Mac said, putting his arm around Carissa, who merely looked straight ahead with a blank look in her eyes.

"Any limbo can only be opened when somebody is sent there," the lady continued to explain. "So we waited as long as we could, watching the wreckage Dvorak was causing. Then, shortly before midnight, Ariana sent Isabel to limbo, and on her way there, she invoked her powers. That pulled you all out of limbo and activated Carissa's list."

"And got her stuck in there," Carissa said, very quietly.

The old lady sighed. "She said she would do it. I told her the consequences of her actions. But she wanted to make sure you got back to this world, Carissa."

"She said...she said to drink lots of chai," Carissa said, losing her voice to the tears that were coming.

"Now that Dvorak is gone, a new replacement will have to be found for Dvorak," the lady explained. "We've never had to do this before. In that case, we need to leave for our dimension as soon as possible." She stood up from her bench and walked over to Mick. "I am so looking forward to all of the paperwork. Are you ready, sweetheart?"

"There's only one more thing I would like to say," Mick said. "And this concerns Carissa. We have mentioned before that everybody in limbo ceases to exist on the fated day. Do you remember that?"

Carissa could only nod. "Get to the point," Mac said, cross.

"It has also been said that those people from the other world who are qualified enough can become members of QWERTY instead of disappearing. That's how Sarah here and I became members. Do you remember me saying this?"

Carissa caught her breath, and for the first time, she smiled. "You mean --"

"We can't tell for sure, but we'll know once we return to our own realm. But I'm pretty sure your friend is qualified." Mick took Sarah's hand. "We must go now."

And just like that, they did, as if they had never been there to begin with. The world was born anew at midnight, and as far as Carissa knew, it was missing only one soul.

Mac met Carissa the next morning, a Monday and the start of the school week, at the Saint Arbucks where it had all started. Everything was normal again, although he did notice that, for whatever reason, the prices were cheaper than he had anticipated. Perhaps Carissa's decisions about their world reached farther than he knew.

Carissa smiled when she saw him. Both were in their school uniforms, and Carissa still had her duffel. "Any word on the book?" Mac asked as they sat down, him with a mint tea, her with her chai.

Carissa shook her head. "None, but I don't have it. I bet it's back in the library where it belongs." She sighed. "I wonder if Isabel is going to still celebrate her birthday next month. I mean, I know I'm talking like she still exists --"

"She does," Mac said. "And she's probably asking Sarah and Mick lots of questions right now. Things like, 'do they serve chai in this reality?' Stuff like that."

Carissa laughed. "I hope so."

"Well, this is also the first time that Dvorak has been beaten. QWERTY isn't playing by the rules anymore, so if anybody can find a way to come back to this realm, I guarantee it's Isabel. Even if it's just to get some chai."

"Yeah, but nobody would recognize her." That was true; while Isabel's parents were still lifelong friends of the Lopezes, they had all of their sons and daughters save for one, and to them, it had always been this way.

"You and I remember her. And your parents, and Peter. He called, by the way. He's gonna take today off school. I think staying in limbo for all that time can do a doozy on your brain."

"Funny," Carissa said as she rolled her eyes. "Do you think we can still have a party for Isabel?"

"Of course. With lots of red balloons and everything. We'll get her presents, and when she finds a way to come back, we'll give them to her. Even if it takes years."

Carissa forced a smile on her face. "Even if it takes years."

"Now." Mac leaned on his hands and stared at Carissa.

"Was that line about the chai the only message Isabel had for you before trading places?"

Carissa blushed. "What's that supposed to mean?"

"Don't play games with me. I heard what she said. And I think it's a noble pursuit."

Carissa could only stare back in shock. "You mean this is...a DTR at the Saint Arbucks?"

Mac looked back in confusion. "What?"

"Define the relationship. Are we friends, or are we..." She waved her hand around in midair. "You know."

Mac waved his hand around in midair as well. "I think we're much more than this." And he leaned forward and kissed her cheek. "We'll work it out. And I don't want to work it out with anybody but you." He reached into his wallet and pulled out a card, showing it to Carissa. "And you know why."

"I do," Carissa said with a smile as she looked at Mac's new Social Security card with his name on it. "Your mother has hers, too, I assume?"

"She does. Applying for schools now will be so much easier."

"As long as you go to school here in the city, I'm game."

They smiled at each other, then downed the rest of their

drinks and headed to school, where nothing had changed. Everybody was running around, getting to their classes. "You know," Carissa said as she put her duffel in her locker, "I'm never going to be able to see reality the same way again."

"That's because it's not," Mac answered with a smile. "You changed a lot of things when you wrote that book. But it's not just you. I think everybody has a little bit of power, if not to change the world, then to at least change theirs --"

"Carissa!"

Mac's philosophical speech was interrupted by a glomp hug from behind Carissa. Carissa tried to move away from her attacker, and when she finally did, she didn't recognize the girl. She was blonde haired and brown eyed, with fair skin and a pink backpack on her shoulders. Her version of the school uniform included knee high penguin socks...socks that, if Carissa remembered correctly, weren't allowed. Unless that was something she had written in the book?

"Girl," the blonde haired girl said, "you didn't wait for me this morning! What's up with that? We were doing so good with our record, too, and I was kind of hoping we could keep it going for three weeks, but no, you didn't show up at the front of the school like you always do, and I tried looking for you at Saint Arbucks but you may have been sitting in the back and I had to get to class --" She stopped and saw Mac. "No way. No way! Carissa Lopez and Mac Taggart, the school genius!" The girl squealed. "I can't believe it! You should have told me! I didn't know anything about this. And you know I know everything about you! Why didn't I hear about this, like, last week! When did you guys DTR? Omigosh, wait. Were you doing that this morning?"

Carissa had to put a stop to this, sooner rather than later. Whoever this girl was, she was making her head spin. "Hold on just a moment. Are you new here or something?"

The blonde girl looked hurt. "Seriously, Carissa, what was in your chai this morning?" she asked.

Mac put his hand on Carissa's shoulder. "Carissa..."

"No, Mac." Carissa had had enough with reality for the next millennium or so. She turned back to the mystery girl. She wanted answers, and she wanted them now. "I've had a long weekend that you wouldn't even believe. I just want your name, and then I'll leave you alone and you should do the same."

"Uh, all right. I'm Isabelle Plotnikov, your bestest friend, like, ever. We've lived in the same building since we were kids and my family moved to Washington Heights from Brighton. And we went to the same elementary school. Spirit sisters. Remember?"

And it all made sense. For what was missing in one world needed to be replaced, and balance needed to be kept. Carissa wasn't sure if this Isabelle would ever understand, but she knew her Isabel would.

"Yes," she said. "I remember."

d-VOR-ak

The Saga Continues!

The interactive adventure continues every Friday!
Read along with the serial and comment with what you
think should happen next.

whatisdvorak.emilyannimes.com

for arc summaries, short stories, interviews, and every
Friday's update!

Book 0: Dvorak Classic

Now available in print!

*Carissa Lopez and her friends are the only ones who can
save their world in this science fiction string theory
serialization.*

Book 1: The Dealey Five

Began Serialization May 31, 2013

*Their world was destroyed in Dvorak Classic. Now, five kids must
band together to fulfill their destiny as members of QWERTY and
save the world...wait. Actually, I wouldn't trust those five with
ANYTHING.*

Book 2: *Insert Title Here*

Begins Serialization December 28, 2013!!

Emily Ann Imes is a connoisseur of words, a roller coaster enthusiast, a broadcast disc jockey, a fierce warrior of power and light, and a musician who performs in color. She has lived most of her life up to this point in the Midwest, driving through cornfields, inspiring others to create to their highest potential, and stopping at every amusement park along the way. After receiving her bachelor's degree in music from Miami University in Oxford, Ohio, she spent a year and a half pretending to work a desk job until coming to the realization that she wanted to be an author.

Her short story "Desynthesized" was an honorable mention in the 2010 Y-City Writers Conference Contest, and her novel "The Mystery of Taconum Carnival" was a quarterfinalist in the Amazon Breakthrough Novel Award. She has crossed the finish line of National Novel Writing Month eight times. Her self-released album "Almond Dust" is available on iTunes.

Emily's many adventures have led her to New York City, where she now resides with her pet cactus, her trusty laptop, and her muse to guide her. She spends what little free time she has left taking long walks in the park, shopping, and drinking way too much soda.

And who are we to choose our paths for us?
For we are simply trains on some sort of track on life. We cannot
choose where we go, it is chosen for us. But what happens when we are
put on a path and we have no clue where we are going? Then we must
simply hang on for the ride, and not take it for granted, because you
never know when it will be over...